36 front 26 rear

Lessons from a track addict

Riding a bike, especially one with over 220hp, is a glorious feeling. For an adrenaline junkie like me, there's nothing quite like it. Sitting atop one of these amazing machines, you feel as if you could travel to another dimension. It's just you, the machine, and the pavement. When everything is dialed in, you become part of the machine. The moment you crack the throttle, it rips your sleeping soul from its slumber, shining radiant once again. Your eyes focus, your brain sharpens, and your body responds willingly. You command the machine to go faster, and it obeys, pushing further as your will demands—more, more, more!

Contents

Prologue

So, why am I writing this? It's a fair question, and I'm going to tell you. I'm writing this book because, frankly, I couldn't find anything, not a single thing, out there that spoke to me about entering the sport of motorcycle track riding. Sure, there are books on cross-country touring, motorcycle repair, and even how to improve your riding skills. There's plenty on the physics of riding, too, but nothing that really introduces people to what it's like to start and progress in this sport. Nothing for those curious souls who, during those cold winter months, are itching to read about what they'll get into come spring.

One rainy day at the track in the summer of 2024, I found myself with some time to kill. I had just finished a book about a motorcycle racer. It was good—not great. The story meandered a bit, and while it mostly stayed on target, it wasn't particularly well-edited. The grammar was rough, but hey, it was something motorcycle-related, and the author did have some solid takes on certain aspects of riding.

As I was reading, this thought kept nagging at me: "You can write better than this guy. You've got experiences too, you know." So, I picked up my phone, opened a notes app, and just started writing. I wrote non-stop through that rainy day, completely absorbed. Soon enough, a flood of ideas started pouring in. So many, in fact, that I had to ask my Google Assistant to start taking note reminders so I wouldn't forget them! Before I knew it, I was having one brainstorm after another, and I realized I was writing pages a day. What's more, I was having a hell of a time doing it! That's when it dawned on me: I'm writing this to pass it down to people so they don't make the same mistakes I did. Someone who has become very dear to me took me under his wing in this sport, and now I'm trying to pay it forward in a big way!

My first track day was just over three years ago. I knew no one—not a single person—who had ridden on track before. It was one bungling mistake after another.!

I was green—some would say I still am. I didn't even know how to change my own oil, let alone maintain a bike. I had to hire a local mechanic just to keep my bike in working order. People could tell, too! I had that look in my eye, like a babe in the woods, ready to be either helped or taken advantage of. When people tell me they don't know how to work on bikes, I laugh and think, "Hell, you should have seen me!" I've made every mistake you can possibly make trying to work on a bike. If there's a wrong way to do something, you bet I did it—without fail. If it weren't so funny sometimes, I'd cry like a little girl, weeping all over my oil-drenched shoes.

I set goals after my first track day. I went from the Novice group to the Intermediate group in one season and somehow managed to get into the Advanced group in my second season. I've been riding in Advanced ever since. I'm not the fastest guy out there, but I'm in the upper tier, and I continue to grow as I take on more track weekends.

I'm here to help you. Think of this book as having a track buddy—one you might not have yet. I'm writing this so you don't make the same mistakes I did, but also to give you the full experience of what this sport is all about. I want you to understand every aspect so you go into it with your eyes wide open. I doubt I'll make much money on this venture, so I'm doing this for the newbies and also for the seasoned riders who may get a chuckle or two out of some mistakes they'd wished they had forgotten.

While I do cover riding techniques and how to break down my home track, I'm not trying to replace the more in-depth books out there. Keith Code's books are a staple, and they should be. This is my take—how I approach things through my eyes. What I'm doing, how I'm doing it, and why.

Riding is a small part of the experience; I'm writing about the other stuff, the stuff that will keep you awake at night, wondering what you missed. The MotoGP champion isn't going to give you rudimentary advice on what gear to purchase and why. He's not going to tell you what can happen if you don't properly maintain your bike. He's not going to tell you the things to bring to the track or what to expect when you get there. In short, I've made many, many mistakes and have needlessly spent thousands of dollars for the love of this sport. The least I can do is pass along some lessons learned to those folks who feel the same way. I'll do my best to make this journey as entertaining as I can, sprinkling in pop culture as it occurred to me while writing. Seeing as this is my first book, I'll follow the advice: 'Write what you know.' I'm going to start off with some background because you might want to know who's writing this. If you're not interested in my bio, feel free to skip ahead to the 'Track Stuff.' It's your dime, and I won't be offended, but you'll miss some pretty entertaining stories and the culture I grew up in—and how I fell in love with motorcycles.

Chapter 1: My interest in motorcycles

The 70s and 80s – A trip down memory lane

My first ride!

The first motorcycle I was on was my dad's 1976 Harley Davidson Super Glide. Since I'm 55 now, and if I do the math, I guess I was 7 or 8 years old at the time. I remember putting on his wife's blue jeans jacket with a big yellow daisy on the front, and off we went. From what I recall, we took a trip through the Cincinnati area, and I was on the back thinking, "WOOOWWWWWWW." That was the extent of my vocabulary back then, I guess.

I remember us pulling into a gas station, and the attendant came out to fill up the tank (yes, they used to do that). I also remember him and my dad having an argument about it. There was no way my dad was going to let a total stranger get near his pride and joy and risk dripping gas on his tank. Those memories have stayed with me. A motorcycle is not only a vehicle of freedom but also something to be valued—sometimes above all else. It's almost like a woman to many men. I was taught that no one rides her or touches her unless given permission. You simply don't walk up and touch another man's car or bike, or you risk needing new dental work. Bikes, to me, unlock a primal desire to pursue, whether that pursuit is the open highway or racing on the track. That desire calls to me, and I tend to answer.

No touching! 1

The Culture of the 70s

The 70s were a magical time...they really were! And before you roll your eyes, you Gen Y, Z, and Millennials, hear me out. For us Gen Xers, the 70s were a time we saw through the eyes of children, but we also grew up listening to some of the greatest music ever created. Think about it— Led Zeppelin, the Eagles, The Who, The Rolling Stones, Elton John,

Stevie Wonder, Deep Purple, Steely Dan, Fleetwood Mac, The Commodores, Jim Croce, Marvin Gaye, James Taylor, The Jackson 5, Earth, Wind & Fire, and Chicago. These were the bands that lit up the airwaves and defined a generation. I can still remember my mom's A.M. radio cranked to '11,' as we cruised in her Buick Skylark on the way to the...Drive-In!

To the uninitiated, the Drive-In was a giant movie screen—measured not in inches but in feet! I'm talking about 50-foot-tall projection screens that loomed over rows of parked cars, each packed with as many people and coolers as they could manage. The price was cheap, and the kids got in for free. The audio didn't come from a high-tech THX Dolby surround sound system but from a unique metal box hooked onto your window—one that could, if you weren't careful, break that very window. Big prizes to anyone who watched their first R-rated movie from the back of their parents' wood-paneled station wagon, eating popcorn and sneaking a peek at their first glimpse of nudity.

At the Drive-In, food was either brought from home in a cooler or bought at the concession stand—a building you'd only brave after navigating over broken glass, cigarette butts, beer cans, and bottles of

Boon's Farm. For those who collected beer cans, the Drive-In was like a treasure trove. And here's the kicker: parents actually let their kids wander the parking lot *after dark,* weaving through a maze of cars and pickup trucks, whose owners were often smoking doobies and sipping on Pabst Blue Ribbon, Miller High Life, Budweiser, Löwenbräu, and Wild Irish Rose—right out in the open for everyone to see. The Drive-In was like New Orleans for the everyday person. It was a blast, man.

Near the end of the 70s, things started to change. Suddenly, we were hearing beats with a driving tempo that made you want to, well, dance! The music had these strange, infectious horn, bass, and guitar arrangements that cast everything in a new light. Disco balls, strobe lights, and floors lit up with a kaleidoscope of color! If you were doing drugs and listening to Rock 'n Roll, you were probably sitting down, lost in the music. But with Disco, you were still doing drugs, sure, but you also had the undeniable urge to shake what your momma gave ya. I mean, how could you not feel good decked out in tight leather and polyester from head to toe? Nothing breathes quite like polyester! Tight white pants paired with matching white platform shoes, massive shirt collars, gold chains, rings, and wrist jewelry—for the men! I dare you to put on the Bee Gee's 'You Should Be Dancing' and keep your foot flat on the floor. And if you ever wonder why cocaine was so prevalent back then, well, blame it on Disco. For the full visual, just watch the movie *Saturday Night Fever,* and you'll get an idea of what supposedly killed Rock 'n Roll and why the hoods and burn-outs wore t-shirts demanding 'Death to Disco'!

Kids of the Gen Xers or late Baby Boomers, ask your parents. Look at their old pictures! They won't have them on their phone, and they might be a bit apprehensive to show you, but check them out and see how they looked back in the day. You'll probably find these full-color glossies on pieces of plastic paper—just make sure to grab them from the edges, or you'll smudge them. If they haven't faded, they might still be in color. And while you're at it, ask if they have any old 'albums.' These round pieces of vinyl were played on a 'turntable.' Hey, don't laugh—that was magic back then, along with the '8-track' and 'cassette' tape. I preferred albums, but tapes were portable, even if they did sometimes get eaten by your tape deck. Ever get tangled up in your own cassette tape? Ah, you had to love analog technology.

I'd be derelict in my duties if I didn't bring up a couple of movies that *had* to be seen in a theater near you. First up, *Jaws.* This movie was single-handedly responsible for making adults and kids alike afraid to go into the water. That damn shark was relentless. It was like Jaws had a built-in GPS, always knowing exactly where the shark hunter and his family were, ready to pounce and turn the water blood red. (The amount of blood washing up on the boat and shoreline was AWESOME.)

On the flip side, there was *Star Wars.* A science fiction marvel with massive spaceships and special effects that told an epic tale of Good vs. Evil in ways we had never seen before. Darth Vader? He was badass, evil or not. However, I'm still not sure who would win in a face-off between him and Superman. Speaking of Superman, *Superman* was the original superhero movie. It brought to life the comic book we all loved as kids, years before Marvel would step into the genre.

Both of these movies defined an era and were must-sees, showing us just how powerful film could be.

But, magical or not, it wasn't always puppies and butterflies. Now that I'm older, I realize the 'good ole days' weren't so good for everyone. I don't want to be a downer here, but things like bigotry and the way we treated the environment don't exactly jive with me now. I won't go too far down that rabbit hole, but if you're interested in a humorous take on the times, you might want to check out Archie Bunker's *sophisticated* outlook on *All in the Family* or see how they "moved on up" with *The Jeffersons.* You could also watch how inner-city folks lived on *Good Times* or *Sanford and Son.* These shows had a way of shining a light on the issues of the day while still making us laugh.

The Culture of the 80s

Eddie Van Halen…Rest in Peace. 1

Well, the '70s kind of started to fizzle out. Oil prices were sky-high, and there were lines around the block to get gas. An oil embargo will do that. Tack on a recession, 10-15% inflation (with mortgage rates to match), a hostage crisis, the Soviet Union rattling their nuclear sabers (not light sabers, unfortunately), and poor Jimmy Carter didn't have a chance. What we needed was a force for good! To bring back the 'good ole days' where 'Leave it to Beaver' and 'Happy Days' were the rule, and the only menace around was named 'Dennis.' What we needed was a badass. Someone to take on the Soviets, restore America to glory once again and be a beacon of democracy for the world. Enter the former actor and governor of California, Ronald Reagan (and you thought Trump was the first TV personality to get into the White House).

Yes, the 'Great Communicator' had a grandfatherly way about him and could seemingly do no wrong. Against the tyranny of evil, we outspent the Soviets to bring down the 'Iron Curtain' and kept Volker in to tame inflation. With increased government spending, tax cuts, and lower inflation, businesses in this country started to catch their wind. Movies like 'Wall Street' signified the times because, as the great Gordon Gecko stated, 'greed is good.' Hell, Tom Hanks used to make comedies. Remember 'Bosom Buddies'? Van Halen would ask on more than one occasion, "Where have all the good times gone?" I'd reply, you're in it, man. Just wait till MTV gets going. Everyone will be 'Hot for Teacher.'

Suddenly, as if overnight, things started looking 'great again.' Some guy named Spielberg started spinning out movies like 'E.T.' and 'Poltergeist.' The Brat Pack was in full swing with 'The Outsiders,' 'St. Elmo's Fire,' and 'The Breakfast Club.' People were 'Dirty Dancing' and 'Footloose.' These movies, along with the sophisticated and philosophical renderings of 'Fast Times at Ridgemont High,' Cheech and Chong, and Monty Python, helped define the culture for a generation.

Tanning beds and waterbeds were all the rage in my high school, along with high-top sneakers with colored laces. Who was I to judge? If the girls liked it, I was game. All the 'kool' kids in town seemingly owned a Mustang or a Camaro. All the girls had 'bangs' and consumed 'diet pills' for their weight loss goals. Because it was legalized speed, it had nothing to do with it, I'm sure. Guys mostly had long hair, cultivated into what was lovingly referred to as 'mullets.' The mullet is still around today. You can spot them in pro baseball, hockey, and even on some of our most famous movie stars. Matthew McConaughey adorns his blond locks approvingly for all the ladies to see.

The 80s & My First Motorcycles

Pretty sweet, ya? 1

Okay, maybe not a motorcycle in the traditional sense, but at 15, I had to have a moped. Hey, you've got to start somewhere, right? It was a 'Murray' with a Puch engine. A whole 1.5 screaming horses in that bad boy. She'd top off at 25 mph, maybe 35 if I was headed downhill! You might laugh, but a gallon of fuel seemed to last me forever.

The first day I owned it, I was riding alongside a friend when he decided a right-hand turn was appropriate—while he was on my outside. I'm glad the wheels were spokes because his right foot 'pedal' (yes, mopeds had pedals back then) wound up in my front wheel, splintering all those brand-new, shiny spindles of chrome. I shudder to think what would have happened if those wheels had been 'mags.'

That moped worked hard for me—both for delivering papers and riding 30 miles to a girl's house where I learned some of those 'Night Moves.' It was freedom. The kind of freedom that lets you roam the streets and roads, which, up until then, you could only do by flat-footing it or on a bicycle. Using your own legs is a terrible way to travel compared to the exhilarating experience of flying through space and time on two wheels.

By 16, the moped was old news because I was too busy learning to speed in a 1980-ish Mercury Grand Marquis. Let me tell you, you can have some good times in one of those. You might even lose your virginity! After that, it was a Mercury Lynx—a nifty 4-speed manual that got me used to clutches, engine speeds, and gears.

At 17, I had gobs of disposable income from my job as a restaurant busser at the 'Black Angus,' I decided it was time to upgrade. I bought a 1982 Yamaha Virago for $1,000, with only 600 miles on the odometer. It was a 750, V-Twin, shaft-driven machine that, if you squinted really, really hard, kind of, sort of looked like a Harley. It fit the bill for me perfectly, and I rode her proudly until I turned 18.

At 18, I was ready for something that resembled my dream Softail, but busser's wages weren't quite enough to get me there. Enter the 1987 Suzuki Intruder 700. That thing was beautiful—burgundy, liquid-cooled, dripping with chrome, and it even fooled more than one Harley rider into giving me a courtesy wave as they passed by. Unfortunately, after some money troubles, I had to sell that pretty Intruder. It didn't bother me too much, though. I hadn't owned it long enough to get attached, and besides, it still wasn't my Harley.

Which brings me to one of the best bikes I've ever owned, maybe even my favorite. Enter the 1985 Honda Nighthawk 650. Dark blue, comfortable, and fast (at the time), with adjusting tappets (though I still have no clue what that means), shaft-driven, and damn good-looking to boot. That bike was essentially maintenance-free. Just add gas. I might have changed the oil once—well, someone might have—because I sure didn't know how to do it. A man named Robert E. Higdon, famous in Ironbutt lore and a damn fine writer, once asked a legend what kind of bike he should ride across Asia. He was told, you guessed it, a Honda Nighthawk 650. The motor is bulletproof and will run on just about anything.

I rode that bike from Cincinnati to upstate New York in torrential rain, only stopping for gas. Honestly, I have no idea how I made it. I had no rain gear, just a windbreaker. My helmet was 80% fogged the entire trip, and I had no clue about tire pressures. By the end of it, I had a rash from the back of my legs to the top of my back, requiring copious amounts of Desitin for relief. I whined like a baby, so it was fitting.

One day, out on the highway in the rain, I came across another rider in full touring gear on a nice BMW R1100s. He blew by me like I wasn't even there. Me being me, I sped up to keep pace with him and eventually passed him. But then he passed me again, slowed down, and started pointing at my rear tire. That tire was nearly flat! So, I guess I wasn't hydroplaning after all! Maybe I should check my tires before I go riding? With mistakes like that and others to come, it's a miracle I'm still alive today.

That same summer, my future wife and I decided to check out a biker bar up the road. We both had our fake IDs—what could go wrong? Not being familiar with biker rules of playing pool, and wanting to impress the fellas, I commenced to run the table on some guy in club colors. My last shot of the evening was an impressive behind-the-back bank shot. That piece of showmanship nearly resulted in a pool stick breaking over my head. One of the patrons pulled the guy back, took me aside, and told me to get myself and my girl the hell out of there before I got myself killed. Strangely enough, the very next week, I ran into my good Samaritan, and he ended up hiring me to wait tables for the summer.

Columbus and Campus Life

This brings our little story to Columbus at 'THE' Ohio State University. Mecca, I tell you. We lived in an alley off 13th Avenue (Pearl Alley, to be precise). Not exactly on campus, but close enough to all the dive bars a wide-eyed boy from Fairfield, Ohio, could want... and then some. On High Street, places like 'Papa Joe's,' 'The North and South Heidelberg,' 'The Out-R-In,' 'The Varsity Club,' 'The Thirsty Eye,' and 'Street Scene' were all there to defile your youth and teach you proper bar etiquette. For example, standing meekly, waiting for a bartender to offer you a drink, is a non-starter. Good luck with that. Flashing money in your hand and making eye contact will win the attention of the bosses behind the bar. And make sure to tip handsomely if you want him or her to give you prompt service the next time you saddle up... and there will definitely be a next time.

Papa Joe's 1

The 'Southberg' 1

The Newport 1

Speaking of Mecca, there's this little sporting event every year around Thanksgiving known as 'The Game' with that 'Team up North.' But before we even get to the game, we have to talk about the pre-game festivities. These are not for the weak—you will be eaten alive if you're not up to the challenge. For me and mine, the day started at 5 a.m. sharp, heading straight to 'Nancy's Home Cookin'.' The place was unique in that you paid by the honor system. You could even walk behind the counter to pour your own coffee and juice if you didn't feel like waiting. Tables were shared because, well, the food was just that damn good. I've never had an omelet that could match theirs. I don't think they ever cleaned the griddle, and that's probably why the flavor was out of this world.

If you weren't into hiking to 'Nancy's,' there was always Papa Joe's famous 'Kegs and Eggs.' Imagine sloshing through two inches of beer on the floor just to get to the eggs—and what might have been bacon. How did so much beer end up on the floor? Easy answer: it was dumped on every new patron's head as they walked through the front door, courtesy of the folks on the second-floor balcony! After that initiation, you quickly understood why the place reeked of vomit. But hey, when in Rome, do as the Romans do.

The Newport 2

If music was more your bag, you needed to look no further than 'Newport Music Hall.' I fondly recall sitting on my front steps, listening to BB King. Who needs tickets when I could hear the 'King of the Blues' making sweet love to 'Lucille,' piped through the open back doors? It was also a good time to meet the roadies while I was at it. You might even get lucky and party with them—and sometimes even the artist.

For local talent, we had stars like Ken Durr (miss you, man) and Chris Logsdon, famous for packing Street Scene and everywhere else, singing Jimmy Buffet's greatest hits as only he could. And if you were on the fringe and liked dressing in black, you headed to Mean Mr. Mustard's to 'Slam Dance' your way through the earliest grunge music of the day.

For those with a finer palate, you might've tried one of the original BW-3s (now known nationally as Buffalo Wild Wings). The place was tiny—maybe 500 square feet of seating, if that. There might have been two TVs, but we weren't there for the sports. We were there for the wings! I remember they had four flavors: Mild, Medium, Hot, and Wet n' Wild. There was no teriyaki glaze, honey BBQ, or any of the other flavors that, in my opinion, ruin wings today. Parmesan cheese… really??

If wings weren't your thing, you could always go for the famous 'Skyline Chili' and get your 5-way on, with a side of coneys. Before I moved to Michigan, I just assumed everyone had Skyline or Gold Star chili, served with spaghetti noodles and 4-inch-long coneys piled high with onions and finely shredded cheese. Apparently not! What a bummer.

Everyday living for this guy back then consisted of grazing on leftover banquet food, Ramen noodles, and ravioli straight out of the can. It's funny how that kind of lifestyle can give you a whole new perspective on life. The days of comfortable living and nicely planned meals were long gone—those were reserved for when I went home for the holidays. My grocery budget was more about cutting costs to save for what really mattered: beer!

If I could scrape together $25, I was set. That was enough to grab a pack of Camel Lights, hit my favorite bar, and drink tap beer straight from the pitcher all night. I even learned how to hustle pool from the local sharks, both at the tables and by watching their shell games. Many nights, I'd spot 'Flash' a little seed money to get his shell game going, and sure enough, he'd come back ten minutes later with double my cash. Yes, for $25, I could do all that and still have enough left for two gyros. At a buck apiece, I could stumble home at 2 a.m., dripping tahini sauce all over myself, with one gyro left over for breakfast the next morning.

As for my pride and joy, my Nighthawk motorcycle? That thing ran for over four years through rain, sleet, and even some sketchy moments in the snow—without a single oil change. I took it through cornfields, over the Hocking Hills, and all the way down to Ohio University. I rode it everywhere when I wasn't working at the local Ramada Inn as part of the 'banquet set up' crew or serving at events. One hungover morning, my friends and I decided to go out for a ride, and I ended up with a 4-point reckless op ticket for weaving in and out of traffic at speeds I'd rather not admit.

Those were some of the best times in my life, no doubt about it. But looking back, I was probably laying the groundwork for alcoholism—a wicked disease I wouldn't wish on anyone, not even a Michigan fan. So, take it from me, kids: that lifestyle is best enjoyed in moderation. As the wise Dean Wormer said in the classic *Animal House*, "Fat, drunk, and stupid is no way to go through life, son."

Welcome to Michigan?

Michigan? "Hell!" you say. Nope, I do say. Don't get me wrong, we had options. Leslie graduated at the top of her class with a master's degree in mechanical engineering. She had offers from GM, Ford, Shell, and Owens Corning—corporations practically rolling out the red carpet for her. She truly showed me what you can achieve when you put your mind to something.

Leslie is both an artist and analytically brilliant. I've never met anyone who could function at such a high level with both sides of their brain. If it wasn't for her, I wouldn't be writing this today. Honestly, I'm sure I'd still be back in Fairfield selling cars—or worse, face down in a gutter. I still don't know what she saw in me, but she was an absolute inspiration.

Since she didn't have a strong preference for any of the companies offering her jobs, she let me decide. So, I picked Dearborn, Michigan, and Ford Motor Company. It wasn't about Michigan, really—it was more about the fact that I'd have a better shot at finding a job once I graduated. Plus, it wasn't too far from home. So, we packed up the Sentra and headed to the '313!'

We eventually took root in Dearborn, and I ended up landing a job at Ford. Funny thing is, if you work for Ford, especially at the plants, you call it 'Ford's.' Saying, "I work at Ford's," makes it sound like a small, family-owned business, and it gives off that vibe—like you could stroll over to Bill Ford Jr.'s house and say hello. Of course, nothing could be further from the truth.

I enjoyed living in the Dearborn area. It's such a rich cultural mix, and the Middle Eastern food is fantastic. I met Liz, my current wife, there and made some great friends along the way. It's the kind of neighborhood where you actually talk to your neighbors. I know, shocking to some, but yes—making real friends with your neighbors was the norm. I even had access to a garage we called 'The Wilson St Brewery,' where Mike would open up most Fridays and Saturdays. Friends would gather to hang out, socialize, and drink beer. We often found ourselves staying into the wee hours, listening to blues or whatever music someone felt like sharing.

As for my trusty Nighthawk, it had to go, unfortunately. Riding around in Michigan became a nightmare. Cars would try to share my lane, I was almost t-boned a few times, and the potholes—some of them the size of Volkswagens—made riding more dangerous than enjoyable. One day, I narrowly missed a massive hole under an overpass that could've seriously hurt me. It was time to move on, and besides, I had other things on my mind.

In 1997, I finally finished my degree in Economics and Political Science at the University of Michigan-Dearborn. Starting college in Cincinnati in 1988, I guess you could say I was on the 10-year plan. Back in high school, my GPA was so low I barely graduated. Hell, even *The* Ohio State University wouldn't take me. But after finally learning how to study, I graduated with a 3.5 GPA. There's some irony in graduating from 'that school up north' while still bleeding Scarlet and Gray. Football fans will get that.

Naturally, with my new degree, I did the logical thing—I went to work for EDS, a computer company founded by Ross Perot. So much for my dream of being an economist at the Federal Reserve or advising Congress on policy, right?

Ross Perot was famous not just for founding EDS but for his role in Bill Clinton's victory over George H.W. Bush. Perot ran as an independent in the 1992 election and consistently polled better than either Bush or Clinton for a while. When the election came, he ended up helping Clinton upset the elder Bush. I have to take a little responsibility for that since I voted for Perot. I'll admit, I was really into his 'charts and graphs,' and honestly, I'm glad he didn't win. Clinton was a complicated figure—he 'felt our pain,' had a bit of a thing for his interns, and despite everything, he overachieved and kept the country moving for two terms.

Once I secured my job at EDS, I quickly realized that my fast, cocksure way of living wasn't going to fly in a corporate environment. I discovered that I am not, and never will be, a programmer. I struggled with an archaic computer language named COBOL. It truly is as fun as it sounds. I bounced from that to another job, doing the same thing—winging it, as usual—working with payroll systems. This was during the Y2K scare when the world was supposedly going to end if your toaster decided to quit. Who better to help save the world than a guy who cheated his way through 'COBOL College'? Probably not me. Needless to say, my career updating systems responsible for people's livelihoods was cut short 'for budgetary reasons.' Quite a blow to my ginormous ego.

But that's okay. I truly believe that EVERYTHING happens for a reason. I eventually got a job working at Ford and kicked off an illustrious career as a business analyst. Finally, a position where I could use my communication skills and marry them with some—shaky at best—technical knowledge I'd picked up along the way. "Jobs are like stepping stones," my grandfather once told me. "You just keep stepping, learning everything you can as you go. Just don't be afraid to take the step!"

Lesson learned #1842: If you're in a company that allows you to move from job to job to expand your skills, do it. There's nothing sadder to me than someone who worked 20+ years in the same job and then gets downsized. It's admirable, sure, but if things go sideways, good luck finding another job that fits that narrow company niche you've filled your days with. Pad those resumes, my friends. Twenty years down the road, when you're out looking for work due to 'downsizing,' you'll hopefully have a wealth of value to offer.

Biker gangs

With my new job in hand, I decided to go after my dream bike: a brand new 1998 Dyna Low Rider Convertible. It had a removable windshield and saddlebags, and it was everything I thought I wanted. Dark red and black two-tone—a great bike.

One of the guys I'd have a beer with now and then at the local bar belonged to a biker gang—er, club. One Sunday morning, he invited me to the clubhouse, and naturally, I accepted. So, here I am, with my fresh new 'iron,' rolling up to the clubhouse with temp tags, dressed in a white t-shirt, shorts, and sandals. Don't judge—it's how I rode. Dumb, sure, but I guess I had this 'Jesus on a Harley' vibe going.

I knock on the door, and this massive guy opens it. He's covered in leather and tattoos from head to toe. I gather up some courage, put on my best "man voice," and ask if Angelo's around. The guy looks me up and down, growls a bit, and yells for Angelo. Angelo calls back, telling him to let me in and that I'm cool. Yeah, I'm cool, alright.

When I hear the word 'clubhouse,' I think of being a kid, hanging out with your buddies, sneaking beers and cigarettes, and hoping some girls might show up. Well, this clubhouse had some of those same vibes. But at 10 a.m., I figured there wouldn't be many people there yet—maybe a few having coffee and donuts, chatting about last night, or planning a nice ride on some backroads for a charity poker run. Nope. Instead, there were 20+ hardcore bikers drinking beer and shooting pool—guys after my own heart, I suppose—with their 'property,' er, girlfriends, by their side.

Of course, I take the beer they offer and politely decline a game of pool (hey, I'm learning, right?), and I get introduced to some of the men. As I glance at the women, thinking the introductions are still going on, Angelo pulls me aside and says, "I forgot to mention—don't talk to the women. They belong to someone. Got it?" I nod, drop my gaze, and focus on my beer.

I have to admit these guys are well-organized. When we leave, everyone exits through the back door to their bikes while I head out the front to mine. They pull up in two perfect rows, side by side, with the president leading the pack and a guy called the 'Sergeant at Arms' bringing up the rear. It was like a well-oiled machine—organized, with a clear chain of command. It almost felt like the military or a corporation in its structure.

The 'Sergeant at Arms' walks over and tells me to stay 100 yards back from the rest of the pack because 'newbies' don't ride with them. I can see why that's a good idea, so I nod in complete agreement. I could only imagine what kind of disaster I would've caused trying to keep up with their perfectly ordered formation.

We shove off from the curb, and off we go, rambling down the road. One green light after another, making our way toward Detroit. A few miles up the road, we hit a light that turns red just as I'm about to get through the intersection. The 'Sergeant of Arms' shouts something (probably some colorful remark about the newbie), throws up his arm, and the entire two-rowed snake of bikers pulls off to the shoulder to wait for me. How nice are these guys, right?! They actually stop for me.

We eventually hit the highway and spot a lone biker on the side of the road. He doesn't seem to be affiliated with the club, but once again, the 'Sergeant of Arms' raises his arm, and a rider peels off to help the distressed biker. I'm impressed. These guys may look tough, but deep down, they're sweethearts! At this point, I'm already imagining myself in a leather vest with some tattoos and maybe even a ponytail. I'm fitting right in!

We roll into downtown and pull up to a restaurant around noon. The place is open—well, kind of. I'm guessing they have reservations. All the bikers park right in front, smack in front of a fire hydrant. Naturally, I assume they'll have to move and find another spot, but no. One of the guys magically produces an orange barrel—no idea where from—and plops it right on top of the fire hydrant. Problem solved. That's some quick thinking.

Inside, we take our seats, and a jumpy-looking guy comes to take our orders. Beers all around, chips, and salsa to start. The president casually glances at a picture hanging on the wall—I don't remember exactly, maybe Elvis in a sombrero—then pulls out a switchblade and cuts the picture right out of its frame. Well, there goes my rosy image of how "nice" these guys are.

As the conversation flows, one of the guys starts explaining the initiation process. It seems pretty straightforward—start as a newbie, take care of the bikes, fetch beers, and stay away from their women. Easy enough, right? But then he mentions spending 18 hours a day with the club. I started thinking about my loving wife and how she might not be thrilled with that. I mention it, and one of the guys laughs, "You're married? Not anymore!" (Cue laughter, especially from the women.)

That's when it hits me—this biker gang life isn't really for me. With that realization, I just sit back, enjoy the rest of the ride, and soak in the experience of what would be my first—and only—time riding with a biker gang.

Marriages

"Dude, get to the bike stuff!" Hold your horses; it's coming. You might as well get your money's worth here. Besides, what else do you have going on? My guess is you'd be doing exactly this anyway.

Through my 20s and 30s, riding took a back seat. Other things started to take over, like work, hanging out at bars, smoking meat, golfing, and playing flag football. What can I say—I'm a Renaissance man. It was also during this time that my beautiful daughter came into the world. A bouncing baby girl!

Now, Leslie and I had been on shaky ground for the last couple of years, so naturally, we thought having a child was a great idea. What could possibly go wrong?

Not exactly a bouncing baby girl anymore 1

Truth be told, what was once a strong relationship—one where people thought we'd be together forever—slowly crumbled to dust. We simply started moving in different directions. She got more into sports and spiritual activities while I kept pursuing my usual routine, which mostly revolved around friends and drinking. We were both having fun, but we were also living separate lives. Gradually, we became more like roommates than a couple gearing up for the parenting years.

The final straw came one day after she returned from a weekend-long spiritual retreat. She looked at me and said, "Bryan, we need to get rid of the TV, and I want to do another Ironman competition."

Side note—do you know how much time it takes to train for an Ironman? Her schedule was brutal. She'd wake up at 4 a.m. to go for a run, work a full 8-hour day, hit the pool for laps, and wouldn't be home until 9 p.m. Weekends were more of the same. Rinse and repeat. Let me tell you, a guy can get pretty lonely.

Now, I'm a good guy, and I'm willing to pull my weight around the house, but let me get this straight—I get to clean the house, do the shopping, cook the meals, mow the lawn, tend to the yard, milk the chickens (kidding), and on top of all that, take care of OUR daughter, all WITHOUT a TV? The sake I was prepping in Hannah's bottle warmer at 10 a.m. wasn't nearly enough to make this conversation go down any easier. I'm not built for that kind of life, no matter how much booze you run through me. Not surprisingly, divorce papers were filed soon after, and we agreed on split custody. Honestly, since I was already doing most of the work, it seemed like the right call.

I ended up moving in with my best friend, Paul. Yep, two men and a baby—literally. But it didn't take long for me to realize that smoking and drinking with my daughter around wasn't exactly the best parenting strategy. I needed to get my own place, fast. I mean, I can do all that in my own house, right?

It was the first time in my life that I found myself truly on my own, and I wasn't ready for it. I was basically a grown boy with no clue how to raise a daughter. I needed help. What I really needed was… another wife!

Raising a child was a bit more than I'd bargained for, especially when it came to sacrificing personal freedoms. If I needed to shower or use the bathroom, it would've been nice to do so without having Hannah attached to my hip—for obvious reasons. At 1 or 2 years old, she needed to be close by, but it was exhausting. I also could've used a little help for a change. I know all the single mothers out there are rolling their eyes and thinking, "Cry me a river," and they're half right. I loved my daughter, and I knew what was best for her. But I also knew I couldn't give her everything she needed at that point in my life.

I did my best. I took her to Greenfield Village every weekend in the summer, to the park, and I tried to entertain her and teach her about the little bits of life I thought a toddler should know. But at barely 2 years old, she deserved better than what I could offer at the time.

About six months later, I met my future wife #2. Can you spell 'rebound'? She couldn't have kids of her own, and here I was with a ready-made family with one. She told me she liked keeping a clean house and was a Buckeye fan, so in the words of the great Navin R. Johnson from *The Jerk*, "I don't have to change anything at all!" Little did I know that she wasn't as great at those tasks as advertised, and soon enough, I found myself right back in the same boat. Except this time, I had the added pressure of a stressful new job, a growing relationship with alcohol, and a fresh diagnosis of bipolar disorder and depression. I was quickly spiraling out of control.

All told, my years with wife #2 are mostly a blur. She wasn't a bad person, but our expectations of each other fell short. We loved the *idea* of marriage, but we struggled to love each other. Friends and family had warned me that this was a marriage of convenience, and they were right. In the end, the only truly great thing to come out of that relationship, at least from a motorcycle perspective, was my favorite Harley—a 2008 Softail Custom.

Now, for transparency, there are two sides to every story, but since you didn't pay to read their point of view, my side will have to do. Even though my heart was in the right place, and I did try to make both my marriages work, the lifestyle I chose to live did get in the way of a healthy marriage. I just wasn't ready to let go of my youth, I suppose. It's immaturity, really. While I could provide for my family financially, I wasn't able to take that next step and put away childish things. Life lesson 482 – I firmly believe that some of us spend an awful lot of time chasing those good ole' days, thinking that those feelings we had in our youth will magically occur at the next party. It just isn't so. It's best to create new memories and live the life you have now—trust me on that. Enter the woman who would finally help me become a man.

Enter my third wife, Liz. She literally saved my life. I was pretty deep in the bottle and living a mostly unfulfilling life. Meeting women and screwing everything that smiles at you isn't conducive to building good character in your mid-40s. In fact, while it may be fun at the time, it's a surefire way to start picking out a burial plot and getting your affairs in order. Instead, with Liz, I started to thrive. But, hold on there, Sparky. Before we thrive, a reckoning needs to occur.

We all have our paths, and, as I mentioned earlier, I don't do anything the easy way. It was time to, dare I say it, stop drinking. It was an activity that I could no longer control on my own. That monkey was kicking my ass up and down the street, leaving tears, a career at its boiling point, and marriages in its wake. I did my fair share of bleeding at those AA tables, and Liz helped me get there with support and without shame. I went over two years without a drink, and even though I've indulged since, I'm back to sobriety, realizing it's simply not worth it. Each time I would fall off the wagon searching for those 'good times,' my depression and anxiety only deepened before I finally quit again.

Today, I'm clean and sober. Let's see if it sticks this time, shall we?

As for Liz and me, the story is still being written. We've been tested over the years, and it hasn't been without its trials. But it's made me a better man and, more importantly, a better person. I've come to realize that I'm here to take care of people—whether it's my daughter, Liz, her children, or her parents. My shoulders are big. Hop on. Just keep me upright, and I'll deliver.

Liz, we've built a beautiful life together, and I love you dearly. Thanks, babe.

Chapter 2: Track Stuff

A track addiction born through Covid

Put the tissues away, Tito! The fun stuff returns! So, let's recap where we're at right now. We've gone through a few Japanese bikes and a couple of Harleys. And what does it take to end this dry spell in the bike department? A global pandemic! Yeah, we sure got hit with a big one.

I found myself working from home full-time, with the assurance we'd never have to return to the office. "We're so productive, why would we? WAHAHAHAHAHAHAHA. Good one! Hell, I lived just a few miles from the office, so it wasn't a big deal for me either way. BUT let me just say something to upper management everywhere, especially in the auto industry. You can't tell highly skilled folks they can uproot their lives and move across the country, only to turn around and lay them off when you suddenly decide people need to come back to the office (Yeah, you know who you are). It's a low move, especially after those same employees put in 12-hour days to keep the company afloat during a pandemic. You shattered families, wrecked careers, triggered countless foreclosures, and forced people to dip into their retirement savings. But sure, keep on preaching about "company culture." The fresh grads will eat that up. Just don't be surprised when the quality of your vehicles suffers because they're still learning the ropes. Judging by all the recalls, that's clearly a work in progress. Here's an idea: maybe keep some of your experienced people around instead of pushing them out after they hit 50.

It's all good, though. It taught me an important lesson—at the end of the day, we're all just hired guns. My advice? Keep that resume polished, stash away at least six months of living expenses, pick up every skill you can, and, most importantly, trust your gut when something feels off. Better to jump ship while you've still got a job than to wait until it's too late.

Deep breath, Bryan. Deep breath. Now, where was I? Ah yes, the point before my rant. So, during COVID, we decided to sell one of our cars. Since I was working from home, we figured we didn't really need two vehicles. But I still needed something to get around town, and we didn't want to break the bank. So, what about a motorcycle?

And sure enough, I found one. It just happened to be a 2001 BMW R1100s. It was the very same model I had seen in New York years earlier! A hell of a coincidence, or was it? As my years go by, more and more I have found that there are no coincidences in life. You just need to be inclined to pay attention.

BMW R110s - ain't she a beaut? 1

So, I've got this BMW, I joined a forum, and there are posts about track riding. Hmm, what is this track riding they speak of? "Track bug"? "Once you go track, you never go back," and other threads going on about the greatness of riding on a track and how it can be addictive. Wait, something's addictive about this activity? This I need to know more about.

As I start reading more posts, I see someone share a video of this heavyweight Boxer twin on the track, doing things I wouldn't have thought possible. I also believe a little bit of drool started working its way down my chin. After wiping it off, I saw another post saying the local BMW dealership had rented out Grattan Speedway for the day, and I was welcome to join. Wait, Michigan has a track where you can ride at high speeds, daring fate to take your life and/or limbs? Where do I sign?

So, I reach out, get in touch with the folks setting it up, fork over my cash, and I'm ready, right? WRONG.

I'm asked, "Do you ride 'Novice,' 'Intermediate,' or 'Advanced'?"

Well, as you know, I've been riding for years, but I'm a bit rusty, so I say, "I haven't ridden in a few years, so better put me down as Intermediate."

Then comes the next question: "Have you been through Novice yet?"

I'm thinking, "Self, you're certainly no Novice, but what she's trying to tell you is that there are levels to this track thing." So, I play along.

"Well, no, but I've ridden for years." "Doesn't matter," she says. "You need to go through Novice before you can ride in the Intermediate group."

I agree to these terms and conditions and now I'm ready, right? Wrong again.

She adds, "You cannot ride in jeans. You need a full-face helmet, gloves that cover your wrists, and boots that cover your ankles. We also suggest one- or two-piece leathers."

Helmet? Check. Boots? Check. Leathers? "Listen," I say, "I don't own any leathers, just the jacket." "The rest I have."

"That's okay," she says. "You can wear mesh, nylon riding pants that are padded in the shoulders, elbows, hips, and knee areas."

Easy enough. I'll get on Google for that.

With the hard part out of the way (you laugh, and I laugh with you), all I need to do is buy some riding pants. Shouldn't be hard, right? So, I Google 'motorcycle riding pants' and discover there are hundreds of different kinds and brands to choose from. I pick out what I think will do the trick, and I think my job here is done, right? As John Bender would say in *The Breakfast Club*, "Not even close...Bud!"

Then the thought hits me: Yes, I have the bike, and yes, I have the gear, but where exactly is this Grattan place? It's a track 2.5 hours away. If that's the case, I'll need to transport the bike, just in case I manage to crash it. Not to mention, riding 2.5 hours to and from the track doesn't sound like a good idea.

Did you know U-Haul makes motorcycle trailers for just this purpose? I didn't. So, I start looking into trailers and end up bombarded with options. I settle on the least expensive one—a trailer that mounts to your hitch. Easy enough, and I even find a used one for only $100! Nicely played, sir, nicely played. Or is it?

I pick up this hitch device and figure, before going on this adventure, I should give it a trial run. Preparation is key, right? I mean, how hard could it be to push a 500+lb bike up a steep incline and tie it down without it falling off my hitch, crashing to the pavement, or onto me? Turns out, it's very freaking hard.

Seeing my struggle, my dear wife—foreseeing an inevitable trip to the ER—comes out to help me. We soon realize we need more muscle, so we call her son, Kevin, to assist. After much effort, the three of us manage to get the bike upright and strapped onto the hitch. Voila!

So, with everything squared away, I'm ready to go, right? Well, yes, this time I am actually ready. Camping is allowed, but I figure I'd better book a hotel room nearby—someplace called the Winter Inn. Cool place, by the way. If you ever get the chance, check it out. Great food and pretty close to the track. The organization running the event has registration at 7 a.m., and I don't think getting up at 4 a.m. to make the drive is something I want to do. I need to be fresh!

Once I get to the track, I go through registration and something called "Tech Inspection." After that, I join the "Riders Meeting." This is where they walk you through all the dos and don'ts, both on and off the track. They also show a dizzying array of colorful flags, and I mentally try to memorize them all—just in case one gets flown.

We then break off into our respective groups—me to Novice, begrudgingly. Now, there aren't a lot of people at this event, since it's supposed to be for dealer patrons only. I'm not a dealer patron, and I'm guessing most of the other riders aren't either. But there are still enough of us to divide into three groups. The lead instructor asks us what skill level we are, and of course, I pick the fastest: group 1.

After we're all sorted into our groups, they announce we're going to hold class. Class? I thought we were here to ride, right? Nope. Apparently, you need to *learn* to ride. Me? Hell, I've been riding longer than some of these instructors have been alive. But it turns out, I didn't know nearly as much as I thought. After just one session on the track, I was doubting if I should be in that fast group, even within Novice.

The way it's organized, Novice, Intermediate, and Advanced each get their own 20-minute sessions (not necessarily in that order). When it's our turn, we start off slow enough. I'm able to follow the line of bikes ahead of me pretty easily for a lap or so, and then the instructor starts picking up the pace. Man, we were flying! Well, not really, because by the next lap, he goes even faster. At this point, I'm leaning the bike every which way, all over the damn place. Lines? What lines? Reference markers? What reference markers? I'm just doing my best to keep up with these guys, let alone think about braking markers. And that was only the first session.

But I'll tell you, somewhere between the "one gear" drill (where you keep the bike in one gear for the entire session) and the third session, something inside clicked. I started to really, and I mean *really*, enjoy this. I was moving along nicely, dare I say, fast! Before the day was out, I learned how to lean the bike properly, use my reference markers, and fly down the straightaway like a champion. I felt like I had won the track day! Smiling from ear to ear, I was.

But I also realized something out there. This BMW of mine? It isn't the nimblest bike on the track. Sure, some guys out there can make it dance, but I felt like I needed a proper bike for this kind of riding. While the BMW seemed like a great idea at the time, if I'm going to keep chasing this new craving for speed and danger, I need the right tool for the job.

The search for the perfect bike

That's not it... 1

What ensued that season—and the next—was a manic search for the right bike. I began purchasing bikes at an alarming rate. First, it was the BMW, then a 2006 Honda 600RR. That bike was definitely more in line with what I needed, but unfortunately, it was painful to ride. Remember, at that time I was just over 50 years old, and the thought of riding that thing around town and on the track felt like torture.

That led me to something powerful with good ergonomics: a 2001 Yamaha FZ1. What a great bike. It had close to 150 horsepower and just flat-out hauls ass. I rode it down to the Tail of the Dragon and back without any back pain, which was a huge plus.

The problem, though, was that the faster I got on the track, the more I realized I was running out of the bike's potential. For me, it was just too heavy and didn't handle particularly well. At GingerMan Raceway, I was already scraping the ends of the foot pegs. I didn't think it was worth the investment to upgrade it into a proper track weapon, and an instructor shared the same opinion.

It seemed inevitable that I needed a track bike, but I really liked the FZ1. Still, I thought, to hell with it—let's get a track bike.

So, I kept the FZ1 and bought a "new to me" 2006 Triumph 675. I immediately added new rear sets (foot pegs) and clip-ons (detachable handlebars) so I could get into more of a race position on the bike. It wasn't the 'R' (race) model, so it had standard suspension, but she was light, nimble through the turns, had good power for driving out of them, and fast enough to keep up with the 600-class race boys out there. The Triumph felt perfect for me, and I thought I'd never need another track bike again. Yeah, right.

While I had this bike, I really started finding my groove. My pace got faster, my cornering was sharp, and I was having an absolute blast on it.

By the time I found her replacement, I was already pushing the Triumph to its absolute limit. Little did I know, the track gods were smiling on me. A man named Dave had just the bike I didn't yet know I needed. What started as a simple transaction with Dave ended up planting the seeds of a friendship that .

My current, and hopefully last, track weapon

The Triumph 675, while perfect for me at the time, had its limitations. Dave pointed out that I was reaching the end of its lifespan in terms of performance, and if I wanted to keep progressing, I'd need to consider a dedicated track bike. I wasn't exactly thrilled at the idea of dropping a bunch of cash on upgrading the Triumph's suspension. That's when Dave, ever the opportunist, casually mentioned that he had a 2014 GSXR750 he'd picked up from a former race enthusiast and instructor.

Picture a man reeling in a fish with a hook in its (my) mouth—that's exactly how Dave played it. He knew where I wanted to go, knew I couldn't get there on the Triumph, and he also knew I'd be willing to spend the money to get what I needed to do the job right.

In 2014, the previous owner bought the bike brand new, straight from the factory in Japan, and converted it into a race bike. He was meticulous with every detail, sparing no expense to make sure it would last. It has a rebuilt EDR motor with finely tuned parts, pushing close to 140 horsepower at the rear wheel. She can keep up with the liter bikes but is light enough to outmaneuver them in the turns, especially at my skill level. The GSXR750 has a K-tech fully adjustable suspension, front and rear, quick-change wheels, a Rapid Bike auto-tuner, Sharkskin race fairing, and a ton of other upgrades that turned a stock machine into a bonafide race bike. Me, on a race bike—I still can't quite believe it.

When Dave delivered the Suzuki to me at the track, I was completely awestruck. The bike was stunningly beautiful and looked wickedly fast. Dark sapphire blue, with matching race plastics. Apart from the previous owner's race number, it was immaculate, certainly well beyond my skill level. I paid a lot for it, but considering the tens of thousands that went into building it, it felt like a steal. Funny enough, Dave admitted recently that he hoped I would say no to buying it so he could keep it for himself.

I moved from the Intermediate to the Advanced group in my first season with her. To be honest, I felt a bit guilty owning such a fine machine. Dave would always remind me, "That's the baddest 750 in the country, treat it as such." But that guilt disappeared after my first crash— my first crash ever—when I low-sided in the Advanced group that same season. I didn't notice the rain starting, and the sealer on the track got the better of me. In a strange way, it was almost a relief. The bike was too pristine, too well-built for someone at my level. It needed a few bruises. Dave would joke that I shouldn't be allowed to ride a bike like that and should sell it back to him. As much as he joked, he wasn't entirely wrong. I had just made it into the Advanced group and had no idea of the bike's full capabilities. But I'd learn. I'd learn by pushing myself, facing my fears, and eventually earning the right to ride that machine.

Life lesson #2763: Life is short, and you don't get many chances. When someone offers you a race bike and your goal is to be one of the fast kids, you pay the man and hang on with both hands. Opportunities exist to test you. Luck isn't random; it's when opportunity meets preparation. We create our own luck. Things happen in life, on or off the track, but you have to push through and persevere. True wisdom comes from living and learning how to overcome the obstacles in your way.

Most successful people you meet don't look at problems the same way as others. They see them as opportunities to grow. Mark Fields, the former CEO of Ford Motor Company, once said that his success at Ford came from "running to the fire." He leaned into problems, treating them as opportunities because, most of the time, no one else has a solution. So, why not you? You'll learn from your mistakes and build a reputation for initiative and drive. And when budget cuts roll around— and they will—you'll have a much better chance of keeping your neck off the chopping block.

Successful people don't procrastinate. When you put things off, the big stuff blindsides you, and when it does, you'll want to focus on the task at hand, not the ten other things piling up, like paying bills, renewing an expired license, or fixing that broken faucet. There's nothing worse than running late to the track because you didn't prepare and had to stop for food. Then you get pulled over by a state trooper, only to find out your license and tags are expired. Procrastination could end up costing you your track day—and maybe a hefty fine from the state.

Have foresight into what you might need and prepare well for the track. Here's what I bring:

- **Tools**: A solid set of **sockets** and **hex wrenches, wire cutters, screwdrivers**, and even a **rubber mallet**.
- **Fluids: Gas** and **spare oil**.
- **Miscellaneous:**
  - **Work gloves, rags, and kitty litter** (for those inevitable oil spills).
  - **Duct tape, extension cords, chain cleaner, lube, a bike pump, pressure gauge**, and even a **syphoning tube**. You'd be amazed how often someone needs to drain gas, especially when small parts get lost in the tank.
- **Spare Parts**: If you're more advanced, **clip-ons**, **grips**, **knee pucks**, and **fairing connectors**.
- **Comfort & Sustinence:** Don't forget the comforting items to help you stay sharp between sessions. A nice **chair** to sit on, plenty of **water**, and **snack food** (I'm a fan of peanut butter pretzels, Fritos, and protein bars). I also bring a **fan** and some good **earbuds** for music to help me stay relaxed.

Imagine yourself at the track and think about what you need to stay alert and rested. I even bring an **inversion table** because of my back issues. That thing has saved me from surgery, keeping me on the track for another season or two. Over time, my discs have deteriorated, and it turns out I'm missing a small bone in my tailbone area. The doctor said I was either born without it or dropped as a child. I'm leaning toward being dropped—it would explain a lot!

Check the weather and prepare accordingly. **Warm clothes, a rain jacket**, and **spare socks** for a fresh change at lunch are always a good idea. I wear **wicking socks, shirts, and underwear** to keep the sweat off, which helps a lot with comfort during long days.

Think ahead. Prepare. This is a fun sport, but only if you're focused on riding, not scrambling to fix things you should've brought. Trust me—this is years of experience talking. I've made too many mistakes and learned too many lessons to keep them to myself.

Lecture adjourned.

Wait, you do what!?

When I tell people what I do in my spare time and say, "I ride motorcycles on a track," I often get a confused look, like they're not exactly sure what that means. From my experience, people usually imagine that I'm riding on an oval track. Except for some super speedways, there's hardly anything oval about a proper motorcycle track. I try to explain that it involves lots of turns, kind of like what the MotoGP guys ride. Then, it finally clicks for them.

Here are some common comments I get, and my usual responses:

Person: "Isn't that dangerous? You're going so fast. Aren't you afraid of getting hurt or dying?"

Me: "Of course, I'm not delusional. It's dangerous, but it's actually safer than riding on the street. On the track, I don't have to worry about cars sharing my lane, pulling out in front of me, dogs chasing me, or getting hit while sitting at a stoplight."

Person: "How could you risk everything, especially your family, for a hobby?"

Me: "It's good for me, and honestly, it's fun as hell! It keeps me motivated to stay in shape, keeps me sharp, and makes me happy."

Person: "Does your wife and family approve of this?"

Me: "Yes, it makes me happy, and believe me, they prefer me happy. Anything else just leads to trouble."

Person: "What's it like to ride like that?"

Me: "It's amazing! Think of it like being on a roller coaster, but you're the one in control."

Person: "That sounds so cool. I wish I could do that."

Me: "Dude, you totally can! 100%!"

Person: "Isn't it expensive?"

Me: "That's all relative, really. Every hobby comes with costs. If you've got the will, you'll find a way."

Conversations like this can be difficult because most people fixate on the dangers. Sure, it can be dangerous. I've seen people get seriously hurt, but I also know plenty who have never crashed or have walked away without long-term damage. If we all knew we'd end up dead or permanently injured, no one would do it.

Of course, we're afraid of getting hurt or dying. We're not idiots—well, most of us aren't. We may have a screw loose somewhere, but as far as I know, there's no law against that. From what I've seen, people who ride like this are drawn to something that sharpens their focus and has a bit of danger to it. For me, it's the adrenaline and endorphins. But more than that, it's about chasing that perfect lap as fast as possible

If I had to compare it to something like golf, a great lap, where I hit every corner perfectly, is like making "Par." If I manage a faster lap, that's a "Birdie." And if I do all that while passing a few people, then I've got myself an "Eagle." A hole-in-one for me? That would be hitting every turn, nailing a fast lap, passing a few people, all followed by a belly full of BBQ and my wife waiting in the trailer at the end of the day. Now, that's perfection.

My family has been incredibly supportive of my hobby, but I've also made sure to increase my life insurance accordingly—just in case. They understand the joy I get from the sport, and that means a lot to me. I always try to be as safe as possible by taking care of myself and my bike, which helps reduce the risk. When I'm on the track, I take calculated risks based on the information I have in that moment.

What most people don't realize is how much goes into riding well on the track. It's not just about hopping on a bike and twisting the throttle. Your "head, shoulders, knees, and toes," along with your arms, hands, fingers, hips, legs, and feet all need to operate independently yet in

41

perfect harmony. Everything has to be in rhythm to navigate each corner and straightaway as quickly as possible, all while dealing with outside factors like track conditions and the unpredictable actions of other riders.

It takes a lot of mental and physical strength to pull this off, using the natural abilities we've all been given. Just because you're great at riding on the street doesn't mean those skills will automatically transfer to the track. You don't encounter the same kind of conditions on the street, not even close. These tracks are designed to challenge your mind and make things feel more difficult than they really are. Most of us don't ride on the street in full leathers, baking in the sun, with our core temperatures rising as we push ourselves through these intense 20-minute sessions. On the street, you rarely have to think about how much hydration or fuel your body needs to stay at peak performance, both mentally and physically.

Your ego and competitive nature also have to be put in check. Pushing beyond your mental limits will almost certainly land you, and your bike, in a heap. Do you know how tough that is for some people? It's something I struggle with all the time. When someone blazes past me on the track, my instinct is to catch them, but when I try, my timing slips, my lines get inconsistent, and I start blowing corners. When your mind is screaming, "Go faster!" you actually need to step back and admire what that rider is doing. Study their grace and precision. Focus on riding your ride, and improving your skills bit by bit. If you do that, someday others might be in awe of your ability, just like you were once in awe of theirs.

Chapter 3: Track Life

Track Days

Always remember, a track day is *your* day. It's just you and your bike—nothing else matters. I see the track as a place free from life's distractions. Out there, all you need to focus on is taking care of yourself and your machine. For me, it's like going on a camping trip, but with a huge rush of adrenaline. You can make it a solo journey or meet friends along the way. That part is entirely up to you.

Trailer Life

I mentioned earlier about my trailer hitch ramp setup. Well, it didn't take long for that to go back up on Facebook Marketplace. Liz spotted a nice pull-along trailer, and I knew it was time for an upgrade. It definitely did the job and was fine for the Triumph, but it just didn't feel right for a race bike. Honestly, if I never have to use ratchet straps again, it'll be too soon.

After a year and a half of listening to Dave give me grief for not having an enclosed trailer, I finally decided to pull the trigger—and I'm glad I did. It's small by track standards, just a 6x12 single axle, but it's simple and effective. That simplicity has become my mantra with everything else going on, both at the track and in life.

Dave helped me install Pitbull's TRS (Trailer Restraint System) for the bike, and let me tell you, if you're used to strapping your bike down, it's a game changer. You just attach the bracket to the rear wheel axle, ride up the trailer into the floor mounts, and click into the TRS floor clamps. That's it. So easy. Shout-out to Pitbull for understanding the struggle—because it's real—and coming up with a solution for us weekend racer wannabes.

We also put in a couple of outlets to run a portable A/C and power up the trailer. I'd recommend adding some wall racks too, so you can hang your suit, wheel stands, and anything else that needs a hook. It's the little things that make all the difference.

A lot of the riders and staff I've met over the years have these massive toy haulers—complete with sleeping quarters, kitchens, showers, and even big-screen TVs. It's basically a house on wheels. One day, maybe I'll look into one, but right now, I don't have the money or the patience for all of that. The idea of having to deal with gray water, black water, clean water, plus all the other things that could go wrong, just feels like a headache waiting to happen. Not to mention the extra costs. For now, my simple trailer suits me just fine. I hitch it up and go. It sure beats sleeping in my Explorer, and it's a lot faster than loading and strapping the bike down on my old pull-along trailer.

That previous trailer did the job, but for what I need now, a regular enclosed trailer kills two birds with one stone. It gives me a space to store my bike, tools, and gear, and also provides a comfortable place to sleep with A/C and heat. That's something you'll really appreciate when it's freezing in the spring or scorching hot in the summer. Trust me, shivering in 40-degree temps in April or sweating through a summer night doesn't exactly set you up for a good night's rest before a big track day.

Preparation

Preparation is everything. We always call about two weeks ahead to secure our usual garage spots. Having shelter, space, and preferably power is essential for keeping your bike—and your sanity—intact. Working out of a parking lot in the blazing sun, even with a canopy, can turn a track day into misery. And don't even get me started on rainstorms. It's almost guaranteed that you'll face one at some point. Ever chased down a canopy in 50 mph winds because you didn't secure it properly? Yeah, that's great fun.

I try to get to the track the night before so I can unload and get things set up at a comfortable pace. If it's a new track, I might even walk it, chat with some folks, or lend a hand to someone who needs help. That's a good way to make an acquaintance—spot the lone person struggling with their bike and give them a hand.

Once I'm there, I like to get the bike and garage fully set up for the next day.

Bike on the stands? Check.

Tires wrapped? Check.

Battery charger plugged in? Check.

Gas and tools ready? Check.

Small table for my helmet and gloves? Check.

Case of water? Check.

Snacks? Check.

Fan plugged in? Check.

Everything's in place, and I'm ready to go for tomorrow.

With the garage set up, it's time to get my trailer sorted since it doubles as my sleeping quarters for the weekend. I run an extension cord from the garage because having access to power is way easier (and cheaper) than relying on my generator, which constantly needs gas and monitoring. Once I've got power, I can blow up my air mattress and start charging all the essentials. Oh, and I can't forget to charge my suit! I've ridden on the track without it being charged—risky, I know—but considering what we're doing out here, what's one more risk? Not the smartest move, but hey, I'd probably do it again without thinking too hard about it.

By now, it's around 9 p.m., and I'm already thinking about bed because 6 a.m. comes fast. Between the drive and a pit stop at an all-you-can-eat sushi joint (yes, I had two bowls of chocolate ice cream), I'm content but definitely wiped out. I have a bedtime ritual. At 55, almost everything I do feels like a ritual. From my 5 a.m. wake-up calls for the gym, to my workday routine, dinner, TV time, and my usual 9 p.m. bedtime—it's all about efficiency. I'm definitely a creature of habit.

Before bed, I like to read, usually on my Kindle. I can usually manage about 20 minutes before I start nodding off. I've always been a big fan of Stephen King. He's an incredible writer across so many genres, not just the scary stuff. I read other authors, but I always find myself coming back to him. I've been reading his work since high school. *The Shining* is still my all-time favorite, along with the books he wrote under the pseudonym Richard Bachman. People are often surprised to learn that King also wrote *The Green Mile*, *Shawshank Redemption*, and *Stand By Me*, among others. Whenever I read his books, I catch myself analyzing his writing style, the different voices he uses, his techniques. I'm sure there's formal terminology for all that, but I'm not schooled in the fine art of writing. That's probably obvious by now, unless I've got a great editor behind the scenes!

I've got a Keurig coffee maker in the trailer because, well, there's nothing like your own coffee. Since I've got power, why not make use of it? One day, I might even add a TV in here so I can watch movies at night and keep up with college scores during the day. After all, when you've got a trailer, why not make it feel a little like home?

Rise And Shine!

Since registration is at 7 a.m., I'm up by 6. Honestly, I feel like there should be a bugler up in the tower, blaring out "Reveille." At my age, I don't exactly leap into the day. I prefer a slow rise from whatever restful slumber I managed to get, checking first to see if I've pulled a muscle while sleeping. Laugh if you want, but I've pulled muscles doing the simplest things—putting on a shirt, leaning against a wall, even sneezing. It's brutal. More pickle juice, I say. Potassium is my best friend.

Now, if you're the type who likes to sleep in, more power to you. But just know that by 7 a.m., Owen will be on the loudspeaker, ready or not, announcing: "Registration is now open." That's your wake-up call.

I'll roll out of bed, slip into my trusty sandals, which I pretty much live in for the next couple of days. They're easy to get on and off, which comes in handy when it's time to peel off those boots after each session. Few things feel better than cooling off by slipping out of those boots. I also make sure to throw on a fresh shirt—at least, if you're not planning to shower right away. If you have wet wipes, give yourself a quick wipe-down. I don't shower first thing at the track, so this helps with the overnight grime. Cleanliness is next to godliness, right? We do what we can.

I like to take a walk around the paddock and track area before everyone gets up and things get busy. At Grattan, the sunrises are breathtaking. The mist drifting from the forest over turns 1-4 gives the place a mysterious, almost eerie feel. It would be spooky if it weren't for the calming sounds of birds and crickets harmonizing in the background.

Of course, the first order of business is coffee, so I get the Keurig going. While that brews, I head to the facilities to clean up a bit and slowly stroll into the garage, which, for the weekend, doubles as my own personal spa. Mornings are my time to find peace—it helps me focus on my riding. Nothing throws off your day on the track like a cluttered mind. Relax, reeeelaaaax... ohhhmmmm.

If something's not right, and you're going to miss the first session, it's okay! Really, no big deal. You won't get penalized or judged for it. It's better to take the time and clear your head than rush onto the track full of stress. Riding while distracted is a quick way for bad things to happen. You want to remember your track day as fun, not as the day you crashed in a sweeper at 80 mph because your mind was elsewhere.

When you're new to the sport, it's all about the physical—your nerves are high, and you're not used to all the things that go into riding on the track. But as you progress, it becomes more mental than physical. Just as you take care of your body, you've got to take care of your mind. Your body becomes a tool to get you where you want to go, so have peace in your heart. Breathe.

The early part of the day is a good time to start thinking about the track. Before I head to a new one, I usually download a digital copy of the track layout and print it out. I try to visualize the lines I'll take at each corner, how to set up for the next one. It's a good way to familiarize (or re-familiarize) yourself with the track. This is also the time to check your bike—make sure everything's tight, like clip-ons, brake levers, and clutch levers. Anything that needs to be adjusted or tightened, do it now.

After that, I'll stretch out on my inversion table, listen to a few satisfying cracks and pops, then move on to some light yoga on my floor mat. Nothing too intense—just basic stretches, unlike Jeremy with his "hot yoga" routine.

Once I've had my coffee and said my good mornings to folks around the paddock, it's time to head to registration. Just need to remember my ID. On the way, Joe usually hands me a banana—fuel for the day ahead. After that, it's straight to the bike for tech inspection. They'll ask the usual, like what coolant I'm using. "Engine Ice," of course—no antifreeze allowed in Intermediate and Advanced classes. I've got safety wire in all the right places, no leaks from the forks, brakes are solid, and I get my sign-off sticker.

Back at the garage, I mount the bike on the stands and get the tire warmers on. Ready for the day to begin.

Bike Prep

I've gone through tech inspection, got my sign-off, and now I'm ready to ride, right?

Wrong.

Let me tell you why. There are still a few things you need to pay attention to—because if you think you've got enough on your mind already, think again.

For starters, it's a good idea to do a heat sync to warm up the bike. Honestly, it's a good practice for anyone's bike. You need to get the oil warm and the engine properly lubricated before you hit the track. You wouldn't gun a cold engine, right? And besides, there's nothing quite like the smell of racing fuel in the morning! This is also a great time to check your fuel levels. Trust me, having your low fuel light come on mid-session does nothing for your stress levels. And the last thing you want is to do the "walk of shame"—literally pushing your bike back to the paddock because you ran out of fuel. The ridicule will be swift and unrelenting.

Now, my bike needs at least 100 octane because it's got a high-compression motor. I run a mix of Sunoco Standard 110 leaded and 93 octane. I even have a sticker on the tank that clearly says, "Use at least 100 Octane." But once, an instructor insisted I should use 87 octane because that's what his custom-built motor ran on. Even though I knew better, I was new to the bike (and motors in general), so I went along with it. You know what I did—I put 87 octane in my bike! After telling a buddy what I'd done to save a few bucks, he looked at me like I had three heads and said, "Man, you've got a beautifully built race bike, and you're going to risk it by putting the wrong gas in it?"

He was right. I ended up spending the rest of the night siphoning the gas out of the tank with a hose. Lesson learned. The point is, *use what YOUR bike calls for.* If you've got a factory motor, stick with what's in the owner's manual. If it says to use 87 octane, then run 87 octane. You won't gain horsepower by running higher octane fuel. Some friends did a dyno run, testing different fuels, and guess what? The owner's manual held true. No horsepower gains, and in fact, they saw a 2-horsepower *decrease.* The engineers who designed your bike are smarter than you are. If a higher octane would make a difference, they'd tell you, right?

Next up—tire warmers. If you've got them, get them on. And don't forget to check your tire pressures after the tires are warm. You can usually tell if they're hot by feeling the rim of the wheel. When it's warm, that's when you check. I run 36 psi in the front and 26 psi in the rear, but that's with Michelin tires, and every tire and skill level is different. If you're unsure, ask the tire staff at the track for advice on your setup.

When I first started, Dave told me to run 36/26, but he didn't say which pressure was for the front or rear. Not wanting to look like an idiot, I didn't bother asking him to clarify. Naturally, I put 26 psi in the front and 36 in the rear. The bike handled like a pig—wouldn't turn properly, felt sluggish. When I told Dave, he laughed and said, "I bet it handled like a hog!" He was right, of course, and he's probably still laughing at me for being too proud to ask for help.

Once that's done, sit on your trusty steed for the day and check everything over. During transport, things can shift around. Get on the bike and make sure your clutch and brake levers are lined up the way you like them. Sometimes you need to tighten the brackets down to get everything back in place.

These little checks can make a big difference, so don't rush through them. Take your time to ensure your bike is ready, and you'll have a much better, and safer, day on the track.

Check that axle! 1

Check your rear wheel alignment using the rear axle markers located at the rear of the bike (where the axle is).

Lesson learned: my rear wheel wasn't lined up correctly, and it caused serious tearing on the side of my tire. Needless to say, that tire wore incorrectly throughout the day and eventually became unstable through corners at speed. At first, I thought it was me—maybe I was driving too hard out of the exit or my body position was off. Not this time. It was a mechanical failure on my part.

Check for loose bits attached to your bike—I'm talking to you kids with the GoPros. Any lap timers, GPS gear, or anything else, make sure it's secure and safety wired. If they didn't catch it during tech, the track might catch it for you, shattering into hundreds of pieces and red-flagging a session due to debris on the track. Use your tools! The track staff won't appreciate your negligence, and it's not a great way to make friends. I once lost a brake guard on the track because it wasn't tight enough. Things happen.

Check your brake fluid levels and brake pads, making sure they're at the specs needed for a safe ride. If your brake pads are low, you risk them seizing up, as I found out one track day. Fortunately, I wasn't going down a straightaway at 150 mph when it happened. My front wheel could have locked up and thrown me off the bike, leading to almost certain disaster—all because I neglected to change them. Your brakes can save your life—or end it—so make sure to check them.

Check your coolant levels. Even though it's a self-contained system and technically shouldn't need fluid, it doesn't hurt to check. Blowing your motor would suck, right?

Check your chain to make sure it's not too loose, too tight, or showing signs of binding. In the middle of the chain, I like to have a couple of inches of slack to allow the swing arm to flex under the torque load of the motor and the movement of the rear wheel, which is constantly compressing and expanding from the track.

Lastly, clean your bike, you filthy animals!

Clean bikes are faster—fact!

Rider's Meeting

The rider's meetings are mandatory—and they should be, no matter how many times you've been to the track. The event director will give you the latest updates on track conditions, session start times, and introduce you to your group instructors. They'll also cover how to enter and exit the track, as well as review the flags that will be used to keep you informed while you're out there.

Once the rider's meeting wraps up, the Novice, Intermediate, and Advanced groups will meet with their specific coaches. If you're in the Novice group, you'll peel off for some classroom instruction. Meanwhile, the Intermediate and Advanced groups will get the first call to head to the track entrance (the grid).

First Session...Let's Ride!

Reluctantly crouched at the starting line
Engines pumping and thumbing in time
The green light flashes, the flags go up
Churning and burning, they yearn for the cup

They deftly maneuver and muscle for rank
Fuel burning fast on an empty tank
Reckless and wild, they pour through the turns
Their prowess is potent and secretly stern

As they speed through the finish, the flags go down
The fans get up and get out of town
The arena is empty, except one man

Still driving and striving as fast as he can

The sun has gone down, and the moon has come up
And long ago somebody left with the cup
But he's driving and striving and hugging the turns
And thinking of someone for who...he...still...burns

- Cake, "The Distance"

I've started many a session with that song burning in my brain. Even though it's about a race (cars, unfortunately), it perfectly captures the energy I feel as I roll out of the garage and down to the grid. I always get excited before the sessions, and I figure if the day ever comes when I don't, it's time to reevaluate why I'm still doing this. I'd hate to lose that feeling.

Once I hear the second call, I start gearing up with my helmet and gloves. I try to time it so I'm heading down to pit lane just as they start letting riders out. I have a few reasons for this. First, it's usually hot, and I want the air moving over me rather than baking in the sun while waiting on the grid. Second, if I'm sitting still, my tires are cooling down. Since I keep them on warmers, I want them as sticky as possible when I hit the track. And third, if most riders have already gone out, I'll have a clearer track to get warmed up, plus it gives me a bit of motivation to catch up with the groups and practice my passing!

The first session of my day, like for most riders, is done at about 60%. I'm easing my body and mind back into that track-focused mode, feeling out the track, getting a sense of my speed, and checking in with my bike to make sure everything's in good shape for the day ahead. This is the time to sharpen up, get comfortable, and prepare to carve those corners for the rest of the day.

In the sessions that follow, it's all about ramping up, getting to that magical connection between me and my bike—where the real fun begins. Coaches say to ride at 80%, but honestly, except for the first session, I don't think I ever ride at 80%. I don't really know how. My body and mind naturally push to max out whatever potential I have in that session, that lap, that turn. I'm constantly shooting for perfection, like most riders. As Jeremy once reminded me, it's a bit of OCD—and I fully agree. I'm chasing the perfect lap. That's what hooks me in this sport. It's the pursuit of perfecting yourself, of being completely present and locked in.

Because when you come off the bike knowing you absolutely nailed it, you also know that in those fleeting moments, you were at your very best. And that's the addiction.

<u>Your body has needs too!</u>

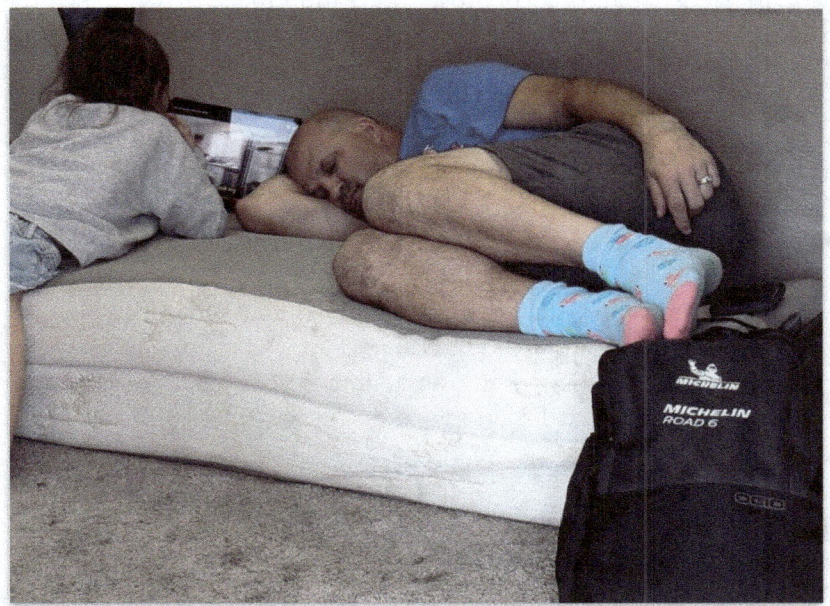

I always stretch well before I ride—legs, hips, back, neck, arms, and forearms. I make sure to get loose and prepare my body for what's ahead. If it's my first riding session of the day, I start getting into my leathers during the previous session. You never know if your suit is snagged on some random piece of Velcro inside the liner or if your boot somehow lost a toe guard. Doing this gives me time to fix things without rushing.

Water and electrolytes are absolute musts. I sweat way more than I ever thought possible in my suit while riding. By the time I get off my bike, I'm literally drenched. To keep up with my body's need for water to cool down, I drink at least 12oz of water before and after each session. I also mix in electrolyte packets to keep my salt, sugar, and potassium levels where they need to be for my body to function.

My body constantly demands fuel throughout the day. I snack on all sorts of foods that are packed with salt, carbohydrates, and sugars—things that can quickly break down into energy. Peanut butter pretzels, cookies, chips, and of course, Fritos. It's a junk food junkie's dream, and I enjoy it while I can.

My brain needs attention, too. Rest is key, and I make sure to take breaks between sessions after handling things like tire pressures, refueling, or other maintenance tasks. I have a reclining lawn chair with a fan blowing on me. I pop in some earbuds, recline, and use that time to think about things I can work on with the track. For instance, can I brake later and get off the bike more in turn 1 to increase corner speed? Can I try a different line or use a different gear into a corner so I'm more in the power band and can carry more speed onto the straight?

Mentally, I focus on staying productive and avoid letting negative thoughts from my life off the track creep in. Worrying about work or finances can lead to bad riding and increase the chances of a crash. Instead, I visualize what I'm going to do on the track and focus on the actions I need to take.

If my body and mind aren't in good shape, it doesn't matter how badass my bike is. I'll get tired, ride lazily, and my performance will suffer—plus, my chances of crashing increase. If you don't believe me, just watch the track during the last couple of sessions of the day. That's when the most red flags go up, as riders push for "one more session" when they're already spent.

Food at the track

I chatted a bit earlier about my Fritos addiction, and I also mentioned the items I eat at the track to keep my energy levels where I need them. You need to determine what foods give you quick boosts of energy, which ones make you sleepy, and what keeps you satisfied for long durations. If you know that turkey sandwiches with mayonnaise, cheese, and jalapeno peppers will make you tired and give you diarrhea, you probably don't want to bring them to the track. This is good information to have.

The kind of food you want at the track are tangible foods that will give you prolonged energy that your body can use. Fruits like bananas, apples, and oranges come to mind and are readily available at your local markets. High-protein items are great to keep hunger at bay, provided they are eaten in smaller quantities. I like protein bars without a ton of sugar.

If the track has a vendor on hand, hell yes, I'm getting a burger! Call me a hypocrite, but I've earned it.

Man, I'm fast, nope!

Just when I thought I was moving along at a good clip, Adam tells Aaron, "Work with Bryan. He needs help with his body position, and he's not smooth in the bus stop." Your instinct and ego will quickly kick in, and you want to say, "NO FUCKING WAY, DUDE!!" "What the fuck are you talking about!? I was flying!"

In intermediate, thought I was fast, NOPE 1

Reel it in, Opie. Most people don't offer advice to be mean. If people see a flaw in your riding and are nice enough to tell you about it, take the advice! Don't get defensive, or they'll never tell you another thing again. People help those who help themselves. John was once asked if he'd rather teach women or men. He said women were the easiest, by far. They ask questions, are more attentive, and are like sponges. They don't have the ego men do. True enough.

Listen to everyone! Remember, they were learning the same as you at one point, so they've been there, done that.

Stay in your lane!

Stay in your lane! I can't tell you how many corners I've blown because I was trying to keep up with a faster rider. There is ALWAYS someone faster than you. Get over it. This sport is competitive, and it's healthy to have a competitive mindset, but if you don't check that ego once you leave the pit area, you won't learn much, and you will blow turns. You should be riding to your ability, not someone else's. You get faster by breaking through YOUR mental barriers, not by trying to keep up with a guy out of your league. Instead, watch and learn from them, admire their skill. You'll catch them eventually as you build up your skills, but you'll do it on your own schedule.

Crashing

Crashing. Thinking about crashing is something that instructors don't talk much about, at least from a mental perspective. No one mentions crashing, really, unless it happens to someone. It's kind of a superstition. Like when a pitcher is throwing a no-hitter, no one gets near the guy and no one talks to him. Hell, even if I'm watching my favorite team and texting a buddy, we don't use the words 'NO-HITTER'. It's bad juju.

The idea is that if you don't talk about it, it won't happen. I think that's wrong, for me anyway. I like to talk about my thoughts and feelings so I can work them out instead of internalizing them. There's nothing like carrying around a thought like crashing for months, letting it fester and get a life of its own. You can't let a thought like that get power over you. I know, because it happened to me.

The first crash of my life, whether on the street or track, was kind of a foregone conclusion, I think. I couldn't get it out of my head all winter. It was always on my mind, weighing heavily that spring. On the first track day out, I was trying to find my speed and rhythm, and then it starts to rain. I simply didn't notice, and down I went in a high-speed sweeper. There I was, sliding across the track, scraping a nice-sized hole in the ass of my suit for my trouble, and banging up my precious bike. I was thankful I wasn't hurt, and my ass survived, but honestly, I was even more thankful it finally happened. If I'm honest, I was more worried about the bike.

Bikes can be fixed or replaced. Sometimes, people can't. Some people, after a crash, simply don't come back from it. Some are never the same. Some won't ride again, and if they do, they never get back to the pace they were at. It can have a serious psychological impact on someone, especially if it was life-altering. A friend of ours went down, broke his neck, back, all his limbs, fractured his skull, had internal damage, and thankfully, I suppose, slipped into a coma. I believe he even died and came back to life! He was laid up in traction and had to relearn how to do everything. He was a mess! But you'd never know it if you saw him today. He looks like a damn bodybuilder now and rides wonderfully. BUT, it took him time and patience to get back to that level. He wanted to get back to that level. He NEEDED to get back to that level.

Then there are other riders who crash all the time. Seriously. All the time! They'll break bones, all the time! If it's me, and I know I have a good chance of injury, I'd probably take it as a sign that maybe this isn't the right sport for me. Some people have to learn things the hard way.

For me, the mental approach comes down to this: If I want to run at the pace I desire, I need to look past the fear. Stop letting it affect me. It was hurting my riding. I couldn't drive out of corners effectively for fear of high-siding. I couldn't trail brake or hang off my bike for the lean angles needed for fear of low-siding. How do I look past the fear? Well, for one, I look down the track. Things are much less scary when I'm looking where I should be and thinking about how I'm going to get there. That spot 100 yards up the track isn't moving nearly as fast as that spot 20 feet in front of you. For another, at some point, I just kind of said, "Fuck it." I started to focus on one corner at a time, breaking it all down from entry to exit, focusing my mind in a way where it doesn't have any room to think bad thoughts.

Life lesson #2831 – Like anything in life, you just decide to get out of your own way and do it. Sometimes, it's that easy. I bet 90% of my life has been spent figuring out how to get the hell out of my own way. Self-deprecation, anxiety, doubt, fear... it's all the same mind fuck. It's only there because I gave it the power to be real. It's not real at all! It's just bullshit! I finally said to myself, "Bryan, you mean to tell me that you've spent all this time, energy, and money, taken other people's valuable time and energy, put your family through God only knows, only to let 'thoughts' keep you from what you're trying to achieve? Really?" Thoughts are not real! Most of them are bullshit, just black water. Out on the track, my brain is a tool. It's there to process track environment and body information, that's all. I focus on what's real, what's right in front of me. If I'm going to crash and burn, I'm going to do it riding the best that I can. Period. To crash and burn otherwise is cheating yourself. You might as well get what you paid for.

Now, I hope that what I've just said doesn't anger anyone who may have lost someone in this sport. I can hear the trolls now, saying I'm a selfish asshole with no feelings toward the lives and families that were lost and affected. That's not true. I do have feelings, and my heart goes out, but I'm not going to let those feelings control me. To play in this sport to the best of your ability, you must shed negative thoughts. My dad once said, and I'll never forget it: "If you hesitate, you die." Stop thinking, start processing.

Chapter 4: Maintenance – You and your bike

Physical and Mental Fitness

Goals

Let's chat about the most important tool you have for track riding—the bike, of course! Well, sure, but it's us, the rider, who controls this gas-guzzling fun machine. We need to give ourselves more than just a passing glance. Have you ever noticed that professional racers don't look like your average person? That's because they aren't remotely average! They are freaks of nature! These guys and gals are lean and ripped. Most are genetic freaks with the size and temperament to ride on bikes that would give your mother nightmares. They need reactions that match the nauseating speeds they're traveling at, along with the strength and finesse to move these bikes around the track like they're on rails.

Check out the Isle of Man TT, held on the small island of Manx, a self-governing Celtic nation whose primary sources of GDP are online gambling, offshore banking, and tax shelters. It's probably the only place that would allow such terror to take place on its streets. These riders are HAULING ASS at over 200 mph. Watch some videos of them racing through the town streets, inches away from stone walls, and you'll start to question if what you're watching is real or not.

All of these men and women are in stellar shape. And that's the point—you can't ride at your potential if you aren't physically and mentally sharp. Personally, I don't have the will to get into this kind of shape, and don't kid myself into thinking I could. At 55, especially with my back issues, I'm limited in what I can do physically to get in that kind of shape and to be honest, I don't want to do what it takes. My goals are different. I'm only going to work out as hard and eat as well as I need to in order to achieve *my* goals. For example, I give myself an hour a day to work out. I'd need at least two hours to get in the shape needed to effectively compete, even at a club level. That level of discipline doesn't fit with the balance I need in my life—working, taking care of my family, and managing everything else. Now, if someone saw potential in me and wanted to sponsor me, then sure, I'd do whatever it took to become the best I could be. But dream on, right?

You can't expect to move up in class or ride at the pace you want if you don't put in the work it takes to get there. I'm not talking about your buddy who's taking to this sport like a duck to water—I'm talking about *you*. What will *you* need to do to achieve your goals? If you're simply at the track to have fun and learn about riding, that's great! You may not need to put in more effort off the track to reach your goals. But if the track bug has bitten you, and you want to excel, you'll need to start making some lifestyle changes.

Life lesson #423: The thing about life is that in order to succeed in anything, you **MUST** try. You **MUST** show effort! You **MUST** make mistakes! You **MUST** struggle! It's the **ONLY** way to grow. If you're not making mistakes in the things worth doing, you're not trying hard enough. Get out of your comfort zone and make some noise in this life. It's too short and too valuable not to, at least, try.

To determine the type of rider you want to be, let's be realistic and not vague. Set a *reasonable* goal—not something like, "I want to beat Rossi." Sure, that's a happy thought, but it's delusional. You'll probably never beat him, so let's set a realistic goal and then have smaller goals to get there. For me, it was to move from the Novice group to Intermediate in one year. An admirable goal—and I did it. My next goal was to go from Intermediate to Advanced in one year. I did that, too. My next goal? To beat Dave. TBD on that one.

What I did was set the goals and do what I had to do to meet them. If that meant losing 10 lbs, that's what I did. If that meant going to the gym six days a week, that's what I did. If that meant changing my gym routine to include more cardio and kettlebells instead of working on the "beach muscles," then that's what I did. I've smoked and drank like a fish most of my life, but I gave those vices up, too. At 55, some things are more important, and if it takes a sport to push me into a healthier life, then that's a double bonus.

That doesn't mean you'll progress as fast as I did, or you might blaze past my goals in half the time. People progress at different rates, and there's nothing wrong with that. If you're trying to get better to meet your goals, that's admirable. Few people will make fun of you for not getting out of a particular group. And if they do, use it as motivation. Believe me, some people NEVER get out of Novice, and that's okay—if *you're* okay with it. There are reasons for that, of course. Some are due to commitment, some financial, and others physical limitations. You just don't know. What I do know is that they keep coming back, and that says volumes about their character. I'd befriend a rider who's out there every season, trying hard and not advancing, over an arrogant guy who got his race license in a year. One rider you can talk to—the other will just talk *at* you.

So, now that you've determined what type of rider you want to be, you need to get real with yourself and figure out if you're in the kind of shape it takes to get there. I had a buddy who couldn't get through half a day of track riding without completely shutting down—headaches, nausea, cramps. It takes endurance to go out there every hour, for 20 minutes at a time, in the heat, putting your body through things it's not used to doing. You'll be using muscles you've rarely, if ever, used before.

Food and Fitness

We all operate under some fundamental rules about food and fitness. I am sure you must have heard that you are what you eat. That's true! If you eat like shit, you will feel like shit, look like shit, and ride like shit. That is the fundamental rule of food. Try to eat non-processed foods, like Fritos!

Okay, okay.... I understand that we all have our vices, and we are only human, but at this point in your life, you know to avoid certain foods that are unhealthy. I personally try to stay away from 'unnecessary' carbs, like cereal, bread, pasta, and even pizza. Check out the calorie count on pizza, donuts, biscuits, pancakes, ice cream—you know, the good stuff—it is shocking, really. I gravitate towards proteins, vegetables, and fruits whenever possible, eating snacks in moderation (yeah, right). I get it, though; it's not easy. My dinner table is populated with my wife's Polish family. Meat and potatoes are a staple. Something green almost never hits the table, which is why my lunch is a salad.

The Gym

Another fundamental rule is about fitness. A body that moves will continue to move. A body that is anchored to the couch will stay anchored to the couch. To my knowledge, out-of-shape people do not perform particularly well on the track. My point is to get to the level you want to achieve on the track, you need to prepare your body to give you the best shot at doing so.

The most important muscle groups that I think give riders an advantage are the legs and core muscles. When riding correctly, you are using your calves and thighs to help pivot around on the bike. You will use them so that you are standing on the pegs, not leaning on the handlebars and upsetting your bike. You will need to squeeze the tank with your inner thighs when stopping the bike. You will know if you need to work on your legs when you start cramping and feel like you've pulled muscles in the afternoon sessions.

Getting a gym membership will go a long way toward helping you work these muscle groups. I have found that stationary bikes can help a great deal with leg strength and stamina building. Calf raises, leg extensions and leg curls are others. I do a lot of inclined sit-ups, leg raises, and flat planks. One exercise that I swear by is goblet squats using a kettlebell. It's awesome for your lower body and core. If you don't have access to a gym, buy some kettlebells and read about all the non-impact exercises you can do. These exercises help work 'functional' muscles, not just the muscles targeted by machines.

My gym routine is well-calculated. I work out at least six days a week. If I want to improve in this sport or in life, I need to be mentally sharp and have the energy I need to take on my day. How many people that you know who live a sedentary lifestyle are fit, alert, and energetic? You see men in their mid-50s limping around, hunched over. How could you look forward to an active retirement in your 60s if you cannot even walk around the block without getting winded? I try to eat right, work out, and stay within a pound or two of the weight I need to perform. I'm not perfect, as my wicked Fritos bill will confirm, but I put in the effort.

Working out boosts my energy levels and trips my endorphins to jumpstart my day. No matter when I have to start work, I am in the gym, regardless. If that means I'm up at 5 a.m., so be it. Weekends are the same way. If I'm off work, yes, I will take a rest day, but never two days in a row. I cannot get to my peak performance without putting in the time to keep my body strong. The gym, for me, is not a chore. I've gotten to the point where it has become part of what I need to feel the best I can, with the most energy, for my life.

Rest

Your brain and body need rest so it can retain the energy to go through the day. Rest is incredibly underrated, and I think more people should pay more attention to it. "I'll sleep when I'm dead" is a familiar quote. I would be willing to bet that guy has high blood pressure and looks ten years older than his birthdate. Rest helps you to be alert and keeps your brain functioning at a high level. Are you sleepwalking through life? Take a nap.

Take time to decompress and relax, even for five minutes, away from work and away from your phone. Walk around, smell the air, look at the sky, listen to the birds. Be in the moment. Call it meditation if you like. Just be with yourself and enjoy what is around you. Bring yourself to peace regularly, and your stress levels and anxiety will dissipate. Your body and mind will thank you; that's a promise.

After lunch, I try to get some alone time to decompress from the morning. I will shut my eyes, and I might even drift off into a nap for 20 minutes. When I'm done, it's like my brain is reset, and I can tackle the second half of the day. I do whatever I need to keep my energy levels up. To me, rest is essential.

For sleep, I shoot for eight hours per night. Why? Because that's what I function best on. If you function better with six hours, great—I'm envious! I have insomnia, so I take sleep meds, including melatonin, perfectly formulated, through trial and error, to put me down, and I wake up refreshed. Of course, none of that works without the absence of noise. Liz, bless her heart, can and will snore, but any random noise will wake me, and for that, my sleep buds will do their duty. White noise only, please. The noise in my head is loud enough; I don't need more, thank you. I always say, "I hear too much; talk louder, please."

These are my habits, learned through living life and burning the candle at both ends. I need to take time for myself, or I'm of no use to anyone. If you feel like you can't take time for yourself, ask for help. You need to take care of you, and rest is a big part of that.

Bike Maintenance

A sure-fire way to get into some serious trouble is to not maintain your bike. I speak from the experience of someone who has dodged many a bullet. If not taken care of properly, this bike that you love and adore and all the experiences that come with it can crash and burn. If you take care of it, it will take care of you!

These are sophisticated machines, and they need to be respected as such. You do not want to know what would happen if your brake calipers locked up while on a straightaway. You do not want to know what would happen if your chain decided its day is done, snaps, and wraps around your swingarm. You do not want to know what would happen if you ran that 7-year-old tire through a corner and it failed to bite. And you *definitely* do not want to know what would happen if your motor blew. You do not want to know, so you do everything you can to make sure it does not happen.

It is not the glamorous or 'fun' part of track riding, but I have come to enjoy it. None of it came easy, and I still make some very dumb mistakes when trying to do certain things. If I lose one more bleeder nipple or drop another screw into the belly pan, I swear I will have to kick something.

Some things on a bike are easier to work on than others, but most things can be done by yourself. When I started in this, I wouldn't dare touch anything on my bikes for fear I would screw something up or make it worse if I tried. As I mentioned, Dave helped me perform some of these tasks, and I went at it knowing I had a net under me if I failed. If you do not have a 'Dave,' ask someone at the track to show you how to do something. It is perfectly okay to ask, and most people are more than happy to help. For the most part, track people are kind people.

Over the years, I have patched together some tools, but I find that working with a good set of sockets, open and hex metric wrenches covers most tasks. It never hurts to have a Philips head and flathead screwdriver handy, along with needle-nose pliers and a healthy supply of zip-ties. Any spare screws and nuts you have? Save them. You never know when you or someone else might need them. Get yourself a marker to help align parts on your bike, like your clip-ons. That way, you will know about it next time. Grab an old toothbrush to help clean those hard-to-reach areas.

Listen to your bike. It is your partner in fun and will talk to you. Listen for sounds you haven't heard before. Pay attention to strange vibrations. She's telling you something. It's always best to catch it sooner rather than later.

Oil Changes

The lifeblood of our motors: I use Motul and swear by it. It lasts longer than most, and as far as I'm concerned, it's the best money can buy. I buy my oil by the gallon or in 4-quart containers, depending on how much my engine needs. I also use a Hi-Flo oil filter, which I consider the best. I prefer the race-style oil filter because it has an end that can be tightened with a wrench. It even has holes for safety wire if you're feeling extra cautious.

Pro tip – Bring some cat litter with you. I don't know a single person who hasn't spilled a bit of oil while changing it. Just sprinkle it on the spill, let it sit for a while, and sweep it up when it's done. And for disposing of your oil and filter, most oil change places will take them—just ask nicely. Maybe get your oil changed there once in a while to show some loyalty.

Now, let's get into the nitty-gritty with some detailed steps for an oil change on most Japanese models I've owned. You can always check YouTube for videos, too. I've seen people work on Ducatis, and man, those bikes are a pain in the ass. Special tools, filters hidden in engine crevices—you'd think, for how advanced they claim to be, they'd design them for regular people to work on.

Here's how you do it:

- Run your bike for a few minutes to get the motor warm.
  - ✓ This gets the oil moving and picks up any deposits that might have settled while it sat.
- Start removing your lower fairing if you have one.
  - ✓ Make sure you keep track of all your fairing screws, putting them in a tray or plastic bag.
- Unscrew your oil filler cap.
  - ✓ This lets the oil flow out of the engine pan. Think of it like a straw: if you put your finger over the top while submerged, no water comes out. Same idea here—remove the cap, and you're good to go.
- Loosen and remove the drain plug, usually located under the engine block.
  - ✓ Just be sure to put the oil pan under the bike first!
- Wear gloves, because as soon as you loosen that bolt, oil will shoot out and likely get all over your hands.
  - ✓ Check your drain plug. Most are magnetic, so any metal deposits from the motor will be stuck to it. Don't freak out if you see metal—this is normal.
  - ✓ Take a look at your oil. If it's pitch black, you're a filthy animal (just kidding). But you should ask yourself when you last changed it and how hard you've been riding. If it's your 10th track day, well, now you know for next time—maybe change it after the 5th day.
- Loosen and remove the oil filter, which is usually at the front of the engine. Oil will drip down into your oil pan.

- ✓ Place the dirty filter in the oil pan to let it drain. When it's finished, stick it in a Ziploc and dispose of it properly.
  - ✓ Take a dab of oil and rub it on the rubber gasket of the new oil filter to help it seal better.
- Apply the new oil filter and hand-tighten.
  - ✓ Use a wrench to give it an extra quarter turn. Be careful not to overtighten and damage the filter.
- Put a crush washer on your drain plug and screw it back into the bike.
  - ✓ Crush washers are a debated topic. Some people swear by them, others don't bother. Use your best judgment.
  - ✓ Tighten the drain plug using the torque specs from your owner's manual—or not. It's your bike. But keep in mind, if that plug loosens on the track, not only will your engine seize, but you'll be leaving oil all over the track. The staff will label you as *that* guy—the one to be watched.
- Now, grab your clean oil and add it to the engine.
  - ✓ I use a thin-tipped funnel to avoid spilling oil all over the engine.
  - ✓ Filling the oil isn't as straightforward as you'd think. Some bikes have an oil window. Others use a dipstick to tell you the oil level. There's usually a line you'll want to fill up to. For my bike, it's almost dead center between the low and high marks. Pour slowly, pause, and repeat until you reach the line.
- Start the bike and let it run for a few minutes.
- Let it sit for 5-10 minutes to let the oil settle, then check the level again and add more if needed.
- If you've added too much oil, you'll need to drain some out.
  - ✓ I've been there. If you have an oil pump, give it a shot, but I've had little success with that—the oil is usually too far down for the hose to reach. I just loosen the drain plug slightly to release some oil until the level's right.

Chains and Sprockets

Your chain and sprockets are the final drive of your bike. They are responsible for putting that cheese-eating grin on your face when you roll on the throttle. The chain needs to be lubricated and cleaned often. Road dirt and other gunk can get on it. And if you have a gold chain, that sucker needs to shine like a new penny. It's a system, so when one of the items gets replaced, they all should get replaced. It's not absolutely necessary, but just a good rule of thumb.

While cleaning your chain, it's a good time to inspect it for kinks or anything that doesn't seem quite right. This is also the moment to check your sprockets. If you compare a worn sprocket to a new one, you'll notice a subtle difference. The teeth on a worn sprocket look more pointed and spread out, sometimes angled outward. A new sprocket will have fuller, more uniform teeth. Sprockets get lubricated and cleaned the same as your chain, but on most bikes, the front sprocket is hidden

71

behind a cover that can be a hassle to remove. It's up to you, but I personally don't bother with my front sprocket.

You can buy chain cleaner and lube from most auto parts stores or online, like on Amazon. I don't have a preferred brand, but make sure it's made for chains because the chain is an intricate piece of equipment. It's got links, rollers, washers, and it's mostly metal, which can tarnish, rust, and corrode. Losing your chain while going 200 mph will definitely ruin your day—so yeah, take care of it.

Here's my basic routine:

- Get your rear wheel on a stand.
- Start your bike and put it in gear.

  ✓ This helps warm up your chain and loosens up any lubricant and dirt stuck on it.
  ✓ Make sure the chain and wheel area are clear of anything that could get caught in them, like clothing or a pet's tail.
  ✓ If you don't have a stand, a quick ride will do the job.

- Once your chain is warm, spray it with chain cleaner.

  ✓ Some people do this while the wheel is spinning, but I don't. I'd rather shield my bike and tire from the spray and not risk getting my cloth near moving parts.
  ✓ Spray away from the rear wheel—if the cleaner has any slippery stuff in it, you definitely don't want that on your tire.
  ✓ Use a cloth to wipe down the sprayed area, getting off as much dirt as possible.
  ✓ Rotate the wheel as needed to clean the whole chain and rear sprocket.

- Spray on chain lubricant, following the same process as with the cleaner.
- Check your work—if it's shining, smile. You've done a great job.

Suspension

The geometry of your bike has to be in tune, and it needs to be in sync with you. If it's set up properly, the bike will go exactly where you want it to, safely and smoothly. You're asking your bike to carry you over bumps, lean through corners, and stay upright when you brake hard. The front suspension moves independently of the rear, with different weight loads and demands from the rider.

I'll admit, I don't really know how to set up a suspension myself. But if I want to carve through corners, I get help from someone who does. It's a good idea to get with a suspension professional—usually at the track—and at least have your sag set. Many suspensions can also be tuned to your skill level and include adjustments for rebound, compression, and preload, both front and rear. Some rear suspension springs even have reservoir settings that need to be dialed in. Most importantly, your suspension should be serviced and checked at the start or end of each season.

If you've upgraded your suspension, you'll want to have it serviced after each season. They'll replace the fluid and check for any damage, replacing any gaskets if needed. I trust an authorized dealer or send mine directly to the manufacturer, as I do.

Loose Fittings

Check the parts on your bike that attach to something, like your clip-ons, your brake and clutch assemblies, brake guards, fairing screws - really anything that can be affected by vibration or force. The most noticed items I find that need attention are the clip-on and components that attach to them. I exert a lot of weight on them and, particularly after a crash, they can move around. It's a good idea to take a white marker and mark your alignment of these types of parts relative to what they attach to. This will help you line things up as they move.

Off Season Maintenance

For those of us who can't ride year-round, there are a few maintenance tasks that folks in warmer climates get to skip. Winter can be especially brutal on a bike, particularly if it's left out in the elements. I can't even imagine leaving a bike outside during the winter months—if you have access to a garage or storage facility, take advantage of it. Here are some things I do to get my bike ready for hibernation.

Gas

Over time, the chemical composition of fuel changes. Pure gasoline typically lasts anywhere from 3 to 6 months before it starts breaking down, while gas with ethanol will break down faster, usually within 2 to 3 months. Most riders will either drain their gas or top off the tank and add a fuel stabilizer to help it last longer. A fuel additive slows down the oxidation process, but ideally, you'd want to drain the fuel from your bike and properly dispose of any gas that's going to sit for a long time. Some argue that draining your tank could allow moisture to build up and cause corrosion, so that's something to keep in mind.

If you have extra fuel in your gas cans, you can always pour it into your car or snow blower. Just be careful not to put more than 100 octane fuel into your car. I made that mistake once, and it ended up blowing out my vehicle's exhaust sensors and catalytic converters. I had my car stuck at the dealer's garage for six months, waiting on parts!

Battery

I run a trickle charger to my battery, and I do it in my garage, no matter the temperature. Some folks will take their batteries inside their home, but that seems like a dangerous proposition to me. If you don't use a trickle charger with some type of internal sensor to cut down the power feeding the battery, you could overheat it and even cause your battery to explode. I'm sure no one wants that kind of surprise!

Tires

Keeping your tires on your bike, particularly on a cold surface, can ruin them. The constant changing of temperatures from day to night can wear out the rubber faster or even cause it to crack. Letting the tires sit on cold concrete can also create flat spots. If I like the tires and don't plan to swap them out at the beginning of the next season, I'll take the wheels inside for the winter. If I have to leave them outside, I'll get the bike on stands so the tires aren't resting on the concrete. One thing I've done in the past is use a rubber horse mat to place my bike on. Anything that keeps the tires off a cold, hard surface helps.

Running the bike

The method of running your bike, without riding it, on occasion is also debated. The idea is that you don't want an engine sitting idle for too long without oil circulating through it. Any moisture that is in the engine could corrode the engine parts, and running it will help distribute oil around the engine pushing the moisture out of the motor.

However, there's a catch: when running your bike, part of the exhaust from your motor is also moisture and condensation. If the bike isn't moving, the condensation has a hard time getting out of your bike, leaving it to sit and corrode anything, including engine parts. This kind of defeats the purpose of running the bike to begin with. Some will say it's okay to do it if your bike is fuel-injected because a carburetor will collect the moisture. My advice: do a little research and decide what works best for your situation.

Corrosion and coolant

Clean and lubricate your chain. You can also check for spots of corrosion and use a cleaner to get rid of it. Some folks will wash and wax their bikes before winter hits, too. Always make sure you use some type of anti-freeze coolant. Water expands and can wreck engines.

Chapter 5: Equipment

Costs

Riding on the track is a life-changing experience, no doubt about it. But if you become an addict like me, you'll need to go into this with your eyes wide open. This is not an inexpensive hobby—and yes, it's all relative. Someone who races Porsches (and we know who you are), for example, may find this to be an inexpensive sport by comparison. But for someone who throws clay or whittles wood, there might be a bit of sticker shock.

The basic cost to enter this sport is the track day (or weekend), a bike in running order, and some decent track apparel required by the organization that runs it. However, as you progress, you'll find yourself needing to upgrade *EVERYTHING*. Clothing, the bike itself, parts, maintenance, and accessories all start to add up as you advance in the sport. These costs can be incremental, but they do build up and can become quite substantial over time.

If you're just starting out, I wouldn't recommend buying a new bike specifically for the track. Instead, use your existing bike. And if you find that you want to keep doing this regularly, you might consider getting a dedicated track bike. They're generally cheaper than buying a brand-new one, and if you bang it up, it's not as heartbreaking since it's purpose-built for the track.

The same goes for gear. I started with a used suit, and all my bikes were used as well. You can do the same with parts and accessories. Facebook Marketplace and track-related forums are great places to shop. It really depends on how frugal you want to be and how 'new' you need your equipment to be. However, there are certain things I wouldn't be frugal about—namely, things your life depends on, like brakes, brake pads, and tires.

Bikes

I've seen bikes of all shapes, sizes, and colors on the track. In my opinion, the best bike for you is the one you feel comfortable on at your current skill level but also with an eye toward where you want to go in the future. Through trial and error, I went through four bikes in one summer before settling on my current setup. I wouldn't recommend doing that unless you enjoy the process of buying and selling bikes—and spending a lot of time at your local vehicle bureau getting them registered! It's also important not to get a bike you'll quickly outgrow. It's a lot easier to control more power than to try and add power later on. Just because your bike can do 180 mph doesn't mean you have to use all that speed. However, choosing a bike with too much power can make it difficult, and frankly scary, to handle on the track. Putting 100+ lb-ft of torque down on the pavement requires a steady throttle hand and a lot of skill.

Some people say to start on a smaller bike because they're a blast to ride, especially in the corners where bigger bikes might struggle. The downside is that smaller bikes can get easily passed on the straightaways. There are always tradeoffs to consider. What helped me when shopping for bikes was looking up the specs—especially weight, power, and reviews—both from editors and forums with riders like myself. Google is your friend, as well as YouTube videos on the specific bikes you're interested in.

One thing that's often overlooked in these purchases is the quality and cost of ownership. Sure, who cares about that when you're just trying to have fun, right? But the reality hits when you start comparing. Some might joke about the cost of owning a Ducati or BMW, and they're not wrong. Compare the quality of Japanese bikes with similar performance to those more exotic brands. Now, compare the cost of maintenance, parts, and the hourly rate for said maintenance. I'll wait... Quite a difference, isn't it?

Don't get me wrong, though—there's nothing wrong with expensive-to-maintain brands if the price isn't an object. Hell, some are absolutely ingenious feats of engineering. Take the Ducati Supercorsa line, for example. It's fast as hell, has enough sex appeal to make your mother blush, and comes packed with enough technology to send a rocket into space. But the entry price is high, you'll need a special tool just to remove the oil filter, and even if you find a dealer, the earliest they can get to you might be the end of the riding season. Great! That said, if I had the resources, I'd still take that bike over almost anything.

For those looking for a great starter or enthusiast track bike, the Suzuki SV-650 is often the first that comes to mind. They've made tons of them, so parts are easy to find. They're inexpensive, don't change much year to year, and there are endless upgrade options available. Plus, the cost of ownership is low because they're so well-built. It's a twin-cylinder bike with enough power for fun on the straights and light enough to tear through the corners.

My Triumph Daytona 675 was an absolute blast to ride. The newer 765 is an impressive replacement, and it's even being used at the racing level. My 675 was lightweight, nimble, and had the power to hold its own against the Japanese 600 class. Its secret weapon? A three-cylinder engine that gave it more mid-range torque compared to those high-revving 600s that need to be wrung out to hit their peak power. Not so with this beauty. Check out its specs—weight, horsepower, and torque—and compare it to a similar 600. You'll see what I mean.

If you're smaller in stature or want something to really carve up the corners, consider the Yamaha R3 or other 300-400cc sport bikes. Plenty of racers and even instructors use them, so don't let the low horsepower numbers fool you.

For larger riders, I'd recommend leaning toward something in the 600cc, 750cc, or even the liter bike (1000cc) class. Personally, I think the 750 strikes the best balance—it has plenty of power while typically being lighter than a liter bike.

Buying Used Bikes

If you're going to buy a used bike, for the love of all that's holy, do yourself a favor and don't ignore the warning signs! You can easily inherit a whole lot of someone else's problems, and believe me, they're looking for someone to dump them on. Been there, done that.

Bike prices vary significantly, depending on where you're looking and the demand for that specific bike. A $10k bike in California might be way more expensive than the same bike in, say, Montana. Heck, prices can even fluctuate within the same state. Scour the internet, compare listings, and don't be afraid to drive. Hell, my 2021 FJR1300 sport tourer was delivered to me from a completely different state! It doesn't hurt to ask. And while you're at it, don't be shy about asking if they've kept receipts. Most people who've maintained their bikes properly tend to keep those receipts – it's just how we're wired.

Below are just a few key questions to ask a seller – and trust me, there are probably many more:

"When was the last time you cleaned it?" I kid you not; some people are absolute slobs and treat their bikes the same way. If you show up and the bike is filthy, walk away. I mean, imagine what the oil looks like.

"When was the oil and brake fluid last changed?" "What kind of oil did you use?" "Got receipts for that? No? Hmm…"

"When were the brake pads last changed?" Hmm...

"When were the spark plugs, air filter, and coolant last replaced?"
Hmm...

"What are these weird peg-looking things?" "Oh, you do tricks on this?"
Hmm...

"What year are the tires?" For more on tires, check out the 'Track Bike Upgrades' section of this book, but here are a few quick pointers:

- A tire shouldn't be older than 5 years – and honestly, sooner than that is better.
- Look at the remaining tread.
  - ✓ Most tires have wear indicators that show how much life is left.
- Check for cupping or uneven wear on the tire.
  - ✓ I bought a Triumph once, and the rear tire had this exact issue. Every time I leaned into a corner, it felt like I was stepping off a ledge.

"Does it have a clean title?" I once went to buy a bike, and everything seemed fine until the guy pulled out the title. Then came the story: "I got a little scratch, and my insurance covered it, but now the title's marked as salvage." Hmm...

"Has it been wrecked?" You'll definitely know if that title isn't clean! Check if the rear end is in alignment with the rest of the bike. I pointed this out to one seller, and he just played dumb. Hmm...

"What's this oil doing in the belly of the fairing?" "You don't know?"
Hmm...

If it's a carbureted bike (not fuel-injected), ask when the carbs were last cleaned and serviced. This is usually done around 18k miles, according to the manual. It's not a huge deal, but cleaning carbs isn't exactly easy, and good luck finding someone willing to do it. I had that headache myself.

Only after you've gotten clear answers to these questions should you even think about riding the bike. I typically text or talk with the seller before heading over to avoid wasting my time. Get a feel for things.

When you do take it out, ride on a main road and go through all the gears. Pay attention to any odd behaviors, like the clutch slipping or the brakes feeling mushy or non-existent. Does the power feel sluggish? Listen to the engine – does it backfire?

I once went for a test ride, shifted into second gear, and the shifter fell off. I had to walk the bike back to the guy! He just said, "Oh, sorry about that. I meant to fix it." You might laugh, but I wasn't. These are the kinds of people you're dealing with.

If you're thinking, "Hmm..." after reading some of these questions, consider how big of a deal that is to you. Tires, for example, are no biggie – just factor the cost into negotiations. But always be mindful: you don't know this person or what they've done to the bike or even what the previous owners have done. Most of the maintenance items are manageable, except maybe the carbs. Scratches or surface dents? No big deal, especially if it's for the track.

Relatively high mileage shouldn't scare you either, especially if the bike has been well-maintained. It's not uncommon for well-kept BMWs and Japanese bikes to run over 100k miles. You wouldn't turn down a car with 25k miles, right? If the bike's been maintained and all the service is up-to-date, it could save you from having to do it yourself. Now, I wouldn't recommend taking a 100k-mile bike to the track, but I'd certainly take a discounted R1 with 30k miles if it's been well cared for. Just use your head – don't fall in love with the first bike you see.

Apparel

If you're anything like me, and I hope you aren't, you probably rush to get all the gear you need for the track. That being said, I absolutely hate shopping, especially if it means going into a store and trying things on. I'm 55 years old, but the moment I step into a store, I turn into an 8-year-old kid, whining and just wanting to get out of there as fast as possible.

Remember how your parents used to tell you to "try it on and see if you like it"? Well, that still applies in your adult life. I know what you're thinking: "But I can just send it back if it doesn't fit." Garbage. You know you're lying to yourself. 'Santa' (the Amazon driver) drops off your package, you tear into it like a kid on Christmas morning, try it on, and think, "Eh, I can make this work." You'll tolerate the purchase. Why? Because the only thing worse than going to the store is packing up a return, submitting it online, and dragging your pouty self down to the UPS or FedEx store. We're all so lazy. Admitting it is the first step, right?

So do yourself a favor – make your mama proud and try stuff on in-store when possible. Trust me, it's worth the hassle. You might even find some cool bike gear while you're at it. Who knows? Maybe a pro racer at STG will help you pick out your new suit – "Hey man, that suit's got you written all over it! You'll be turning heads tonight for sure!"

Track Suits

Track suits… where to even begin? After a couple of track weekends, an instructor pulled me aside and said, "Those mesh pants you've got on will be shredded to pieces if you ever take a spill on the track. You might want to look into some leathers." As luck would have it, there happened to be an outfitter right there at the track. Again, when opportunity knocks, get after it! Or maybe not.

The owner of the track suit company on-site was an ex-racer, so he definitely knew a thing or two about suits. He measured me from head to toe and everywhere in between — wrist size, ankle size, the lengths from my ankles to my knees, from my knees to my hips, wrist to shoulder, shoulder to head, torso length — the works. Since I also wanted gauntlet gloves, each of my fingers got measured too. After all that, I got to pick a suit color that fit my personality. I went with all black, wanting to stay low-key, like Johnny Cash.

Now, looking back, my biggest mistake with this purchase was opting for a 2-piece suit. Why no one talked me out of it, I'll never know, but later on, I realized that 2-piece suits just weren't for me. Another mistake? Not getting it equipped with an airbag system. At the time, those systems weren't available for the suit I was buying, but I figured I could always get an airbag vest to wear underneath it later.

I'm, too sexy for my suit..so sexy, yaaaa.. 1

The idea behind a 2-piece suit seems clever enough. You have a jacket and pants, and they zip together. At the time, I thought maybe I'd use the jacket for street riding or something. I remember wearing a 1-piece suit for a day and thinking it was pretty difficult to get into. This 2-piece option must be easier! Nope. It looks straightforward to put on, but in actual practice, not so much, especially since I wasn't measured with an airbag vest to begin with!

I struggled with it for almost a full season, particularly when I was exhausted and couldn't contort my body enough to fully zip it. Then, one day, while zipping it up, the zipper snapped off in my hand. Well, shit. No worries, I grabbed a key ring and strung it through the zipper housing. Problem solved, right? Not quite. Towards the end of the season, I wound up stripping the zipper completely off the tracks, making it unusable. Bound and determined to die on this hill, I took it to STT's leather outfitter – 'Dan, the leather man,' I call him – and he put on a heavy-duty zipper for me.

Needless to say, all of this left a sour taste in my mouth, and about the time I got the suit back, I called Dave to complain. After making fun of me (again) for my purchase, he offered me a suit with an airbag built in. It was used but had belonged to the guy who previously owned my bike, so it didn't have a ton of wear. That suit was just the ticket for me. The only thing I had to do was make sure to keep the airbag system charged, which, for the most part, I did.

The problem with this suit, though (and notice I'm not naming companies), was that the airbag didn't deploy – not once, but twice! Now, the first crash was a "low side," so maybe I wasn't going fast enough, or the angle wasn't steep enough for it to trigger. Fair enough. But the second crash? I came down hard after being airborne, and I was lucky not to break my collarbone. So, I started to wonder, what the hell does a guy have to do to get an airbag to go off? Well, I wasn't about to find out the hard way again, so I went ahead and bought a brand-spanking-new RST v4.1 Evo made of kangaroo hide, complete with a built-in airbag system. Let me tell you, this piece of equipment is not only lighter but I was assured by a certain pro racer that the airbag is way more sensitive than the one in my old suit. Experience, ya see. I couldn't be happier with the purchase.

"You get what you pay for" is an adage, and generally, it holds true for just about everything related to track equipment, apparel included. When I first started, I bought a cheaper pair of boots and spent the next two seasons grumbling to myself about why I didn't try them on first or ask someone for their opinion. But, of course, since I do everything the hard way, I had to learn the lesson myself – saving a few bucks doesn't always pay off in the end. Sure, they lasted me a couple of seasons, but my feet were uncomfortable and HOT. Believe it or not, you'll end up wearing your boots for more than just riding. You'll walk back and forth to visit buddies a few garages over, head to the lunch line, or make your way to the bathroom to pull off some Houdini-level heroics to relieve yourself.

You'll also need your boots to stand up to the demands of the track. Most riders, including your esteemed writer, will drag their toe on the track while negotiating a tight corner from time to time. Yes, I know, bad form, but it happens. Those little toe protectors better be up to the task—not just for protection, but because you don't want them scraping off and becoming the next rider's problem. A good pair of boots will have replaceable toe sliders, and you can just screw on a new set when needed.

Another feature I love in my current boots is the drawstring-like pulley system that tightens the boot in four different areas along the top, ensuring a snug fit. The "one clamp fits all" design of my cheap boots didn't allow for such fine adjustments, so my toes would fall asleep on occasion. They kind of reminded me of those old-school ski boots from back in the day. And I don't know about you, but I like to feel the foot shifter when I use it—not just hope I engaged it properly! These boots also have air vents in the front that, much to my surprise, actually work. Trust me, wet feet lead to athlete's foot, and no one wants to deal with that. We've already got enough to worry about!

Gloves

As a precursor, when I say gloves, I'm referring to gauntlet-style gloves that also cover and brace your wrists. Why your wrists? Well, think about it: you know perfectly well what would happen as you fall off your bike and see the ground quickly advancing, ready to wreck the tomorrow out of you. Assuming you're even able to think at this point, your instinct would be to brace yourself, extending your arms for impact. It's an instinct I hope kicks in when needed.

Since earlier I said that "generally" you get what you pay for, I'm going to break with that sage advice a bit and say that I've owned both cheap and more expensive tailor-made gloves. And honestly? My cheap set was more comfortable and allowed me to work the clutch and brake levers more easily than the custom-made ones. Specifically, most track gloves have slider plastic pieces on the knuckles of your fingers. These are designed to absorb impact and allow your hand to slide across the pavement if you crash. But here's the catch: these plastic pieces, when they're large enough, interfere with my ability to smoothly move my hand from the grip to the brake or clutch lever. There's nothing like heading into a corner, reaching for the brake lever, and your hand catching the bottom of it instead of clearing it. That little hiccup can cost you a second of braking time, and at 100+ mph, that's a lot of distance to make up. Sure, I could adjust the brake lever out (since it's adjustable), but why should I have to? That's more distance for my fingers to travel, and it's not where I want to grab it.

Most gloves also come nicely guarded on the tops and bottoms of your hands, some with Kevlar sliders and in a mix of colors to match your suit. They'll also have a few different spots where you can cinch them down around your wrist for that perfect fit. You'll know you've found the right gloves when you put them on, look at your hands, and think to yourself, "I could really whoop some ass in these things."

But, like all good things come to an end, my cheap gloves started to rip, and I didn't breathe very well. So, I decided to upgrade and went for something a bit more high-end: a race brand called 'Racer Gloves.' Made of kangaroo leather and with matching colors, I'm thoroughly impressed. I tried another leading brand to compare the two, and for me, the 'Hi-Per' glove fit best and felt lighter. They were a bit more expensive, but at this point, I'm all in. I'll see how these hold up, and if they don't work out, maybe I'll give the RSTs a shot.

What I look for in a good helmet is COST! NO! Safety first, my dear reader. These are your brains we're talking about here. Just because you haven't used them up to this point in your life doesn't mean you won't start in the future! A D.O.T. or other premium certification is critical. This means, at some point, it's probably been crash-tested by a dummy, which definitely speaks volumes to the temperament of the crazy malcontents that will eventually purchase these brain buckets.

I'm also going to see how this thing actually feels on my head. Is it heavy? Does it move around when I twist my head quickly from side to side? Pro tip: Your nose shouldn't end up in the ear padding when you do this.

When I look out from inside the helmet—stay with me, people—how's my visibility? Especially on the periphery. This is super important because you'll want to see bikes coming up on your '6', probably passing you. If you're on a track where you need to look uphill to set your line, you'll want to see as much of that hill as you can. Extra visibility at the top of the windscreen will help with that.

My advice? Try on a few different helmets and check these factors to see what works for you. You might just find that perfect balance at, hopefully, an attractive price. And, as an added bonus, the manufacturer might even make them in some colors that bring out your eyes—even if they're bloodshot from reading this!

Underwear!

NOTHING says sexy more than a middle-aged man in body-clinging mesh and polyester walking around the paddock, am I right? On track day, let your freak flag fly, gentlemen! I've seen men walk around in attire that would get them arrested in a Walmart. **But at the track?** It doesn't matter. We wear what breathes well and is comfortable. The ladies figured this one out long ago, but we discover it on track days. That 'dadbod' is nothing to be ashamed of—it took a lifetime to build that body! **So join the fun, throw on that polyester one-piece, and start the disco.**

Most track days will be when the weather is warm—if not **hot as blazes.** As usual, you'll need to stay hydrated because of the gallons of sweat you'll pour out. Cotton is the enemy here. To avoid overheating and keep some of that water in your body, you'll want a base layer or undersuit that helps keep you cool and wicks away sweat. You can find these online or at most motorcycle outlets, usually at decent prices. I've got a set going into their 4th season, so they'll last if you take care of them.

For the same reasons, I buy underwear and socks that wick moisture away from my body. Most of your favorite brands now offer a line of these. **Trust me,** your personal bits and your feet will thank you.

The hot weather will definitely make you sweat—no way around it. It adds weight to your gear and makes your race suit harder to put on and take off. When your suit company's hangers snap in half or mysteriously go missing, Pitbull makes a great one that feels like it's built to last for generations.

Your suit collects the most moisture and ends up being the heaviest piece of gear. If you can get a suit drier, like 'Hang-Dry,' I highly recommend it. There are also driers for your helmet, gloves, and boots, which aren't essential but are definitely nice to have, especially on those really hot days.

Speaking of 'nice to haves,' upgrades are always fun.

Upgrades!

Tires

Tires are always a hotly debated topic in any forum or paddock. Personally, I run Michelin exclusively, partly because I know Dave—and most riders, instructors, and racers I know run them—and partly because I've always used them. Honestly, I have zero complaints. They've saved me more than once when I've goosed the throttle too hard coming out of turns. My front end has never slid out on me, at least not on dry surfaces. Of course, there are other tires to consider, like Dunlop, Pirelli, Shinko, and Metzler, and they all come in different sizes and rubber compounds to fit your needs.

Michelin Power   *Performance Slick 1*

Pirellie Diablo SuperCorsa 1

For sizes, I run a 120/70R17 front and a 190/55R17 rear on my bike, which is fairly common for a larger bike, 600cc or more. You can find these sizes on the sidewall of your tire. Smaller bikes, like 300-400cc, typically run smaller tires, such as a 180/55.17 or lower. The 190 rear tire is wider and has a larger contact patch than the 180, which gives more stability and, for me, more confidence in the turn. I also feel it allows for a harder drive coming out of the turn.

A 180/55R17 tire will give you a quicker turn-in because it's thinner, especially compared to the 190. I've tried both sizes on my Triumph 675, and while I prefer the 190, there's nothing wrong with running a 180 on larger bikes if you want a faster tip into the corners. Just keep in mind that you'll be giving up that larger contact patch.

For most stock bikes, the owner's manual may suggest a tire size smaller than what's possible. Usually, this is for cost reasons or because it's engineered for optimal street performance—not necessarily for track riding. Don't be afraid to put a larger tire on your bike, but it's always a good idea to check with your local track tire professionals or dealers for advice.

I currently use Michelin Power Slick 2s, which are slicks—meaning they have no tread. When I first started riding on the track, I used Michelin Power Cup 2s, which are treaded, because I wanted something for both the street and the track.

Both of these tires are dual compound, which means the center of the tire has a harder compound while the sides are softer. This setup lets the tire last longer for street riding while staying nice and sticky in the corners. All tire manufacturers have their own "chemical cocktail" for rubber compounds, so which one works best depends on your riding style. A rider in the Advanced group might prefer a slick, while someone in the Intermediate group might stick with treaded tires. My suggestion? Try different brands and types to see what feels right for you. I didn't experiment much, but hey, that's just me. You do you.

Most tire manufacturers give their tires a shelf life of 5-10 years from the "born-on date," which can also be found on the sidewall. If you're riding on track consistently, your tires won't last anywhere near 5 years. In fact, depending on your skill level and the track you're riding, you may not even get through a full season. At my current skill level, I swap out tires every other track weekend. Some Advanced riders need to change them after every track day. At $150+ per tire, you can see how the costs add up.

To tell if your tires need replacing due to wear, there are markers embedded in the rubber that indicate how much tread is left.

One more thing to keep in mind: If your tires have been sitting unused for a while, check their color. It may sound strange, but as the petroleum and resins in the tire heat up, they can rise to the surface, creating a bluish hue. This isn't a good sign—you want your tires to stay sticky, not greasy, for obvious reasons.

Clip-ons

Aftermarket clip-ons are made up of three separate pieces designed to replace your stock handlebars, which usually aren't adjustable. Most sport bikes come with clip-on handlebars, and they can be easily upgraded. On the other hand, some street bikes have a fixed, single bar, which—without modifications—aren't compatible with upgraded clip-ons.

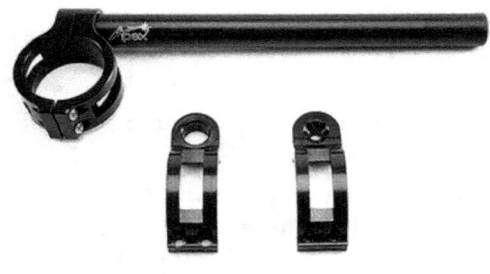

Stock clip-ons are generally not adjustable, and that's why many riders choose to upgrade. Clip-ons help the rider get into a more aerodynamic position, and they also help distribute weight more evenly across the bike. Bikes without clip-ons leave the rider sitting more upright, keeping the weight centered, while bikes with clip-ons shift the rider forward, distributing more weight towards the front of the bike—right where you want it.

Aftermarket clip-ons usually allow you to adjust the angle of the bar relative to the bike. A narrower setup keeps your hands closer to the bike, while a wider setup pushes them further out. Some riders prefer a wider stance because it makes it easier to push on the bars for leverage, especially when counter-steering through turns.

I personally use Apex clip-ons, but there are plenty of other brands out there, like Vortex, Woodcraft, and Attack Performance, just to name a few.

A lot of bikes you see in the paddock, particularly those in the high-skill groups, will run some type of exhaust upgrade. In general, they come in 2 forms: a slip-on or a full exhaust. Both are designed to allow the bike to breathe easier by not constricting the air being exhausted from the bike, and both will change the sound of your bike compared to the stock set up.

For our purposes, a slip-on exhaust is a replacement for the muffler. It is supposed to give you a slight increase in horsepower, but because the backflow of air is still constricted by the head pipe and mid pipe of the exhaust system, the results are marginal. I say marginal because what the manufacturer of the part tells you might be more than realized. On the plus side, they are cheaper, easier to install, sometimes lighter, and often improve the look of the stock exhaust. They will also work with your bike's ECU (the brain of the bike), so there is no need to re-flash your ECU or upgrade to a tuner.

The full exhaust upgrade is preferable if you're looking for more horsepower than a slip-on or your stock set up. They are generally lighter and purpose-built for as much free air flow from your motor as allowed under the law. A full exhaust can shave up to 20lb from your stock system and give substantial horsepower increases, sometimes up to a claimed 15%. You will, however, need to retune your ECU or re-jet your carbs if you have a carbureted motor. They are also harder to install as you are replacing not only the muffler but also the mid pipe and the head pipe.

The goal here is to increase horsepower by increasing the air flow and fuel delivery of the motor.

These are the modifications to my motor:
- ✓ Motor: Built by EDR
- ✓ Full super sport build with super bike head
- ✓ Cam Chain Tensioner Pro
- ✓ Thinner head gasket
- ✓ Denso Kit Iridium spark plugs
- ✓ Ceramic Trans bearings
- ✓ Full radius competition valve job (16 valve head)
- ✓ Surface cylinder head
- ✓ BDK race stator
- ✓ Rapid Bike race tuner with auto-tune

Other things you can do include:
- ✓ Swapping out your stock air filter for a high-flow air filter.
- ✓ Upgrading your Exhaust
- ✓ Tuning your existing ECU for increases in air flow and fuel delivery or a new ECU tuner designed to run with your upgrades.
- ✓ Upgrading engine components such as upgraded carburetors (if you have them), fuel injection systems, performance camshafts, and cylinder heads.

You may also want to protect your motor with case covers. I use GB, but there are other brands out there that look cool and protect the motor.

There are many suspension upgrades. Some can be done to your stock setup, such as upgrading to stiffer springs in your front suspension or replacing your rear spring. I'm not going to explain the technical nuances of suspension adjustments and what they do to the geometry of the bike, but a full race-oriented setup will have adjustments for compression, rebound, dampening, and pre-load. Many sports bikes already have suspension components that feature these types of adjustments. You just need to know if it's worth it to upgrade beyond your stock set up or not. For me, it became more obvious as I progressed in ability. By upgrading, you'll get a much more balanced bike which will be more responsive and improve the overall handling of your motorcycle. Upgrades are purpose-built for the sport, whereas your stock system is generally engineered for the street.

Your goal is to have your suspension in the middle of its range. You want your bike to be stable when you exert maximum braking forces upon it. You don't want to bottom out your front forks when braking, particularly into a tight-angled corner coming off the straightaway. You want some clearance for those 'oh shit moments!' where you'll need more front-fork travel. You also want your rear end to stay planted for more cornering confidence and better drives out of the turns.

A steering damper will stabilize your front forks by limiting side-to-side movements when your front end isn't in a neutral position – going straight or light off the ground – but your bike is. Hence, the motorcycle term 'head shake' or 'tank slapper.'

In my opinion, the 2 top brands are Ohlin and K-Tech. I run the following:
- K-Tech 25SSK RDS Forks
- K-Tech fork extenders
- K-Tech 35DDS Pro Rear Shock
- K-Tech adjustable steering damper

Shifter Patterns – Standard vs. GP shifters; Quickshifters

The standard shifting pattern for most modern motorcycles is 1 down, 5 up. A GP shift pattern, on the other hand, is 1 up, 5 down. The main difference is what your foot is doing on the track. Many riders prefer the GP shift pattern because it keeps their foot from being positioned under the shifter when upshifting, especially in corners. With a standard shifter, your foot might be too low, and if you're leaned into a left-hand turn, there's a chance it could drag on the pavement. That's something you really don't want to happen.

A GP shift pattern is the preferred choice for professional and Advanced riders, and it's also my personal preference. My GSXR came pre-set for GP shifting, so I just had to adjust to it. It was awkward at first, but once I got the hang of it, I saw the benefits. I have to say, I really do like the GP setup better. When you're flying down the straightaway, pushing down on the shifter just feels more natural.

A Quick Shifter is another handy upgrade—it lets you upshift or downshift without needing to pull in the clutch. Most quick shifters also come with an 'auto-blip' feature that raises the engine's RPMs, essentially rev-matching when downshifting electronically. This blip matches the engine speed to the transmission's speed for the gear you're shifting into.Brakes

Now, onto braking systems.

Most bikes today, especially those over 400cc, come with a setup that includes 1 rear brake caliper and 2 front calipers. The calipers house pistons that squeeze the brake pads against the rotor attached to the wheel, slowing the bike.

Some systems also feature ABS (Anti-lock Braking System), which prevents the wheels from locking up while slowing down. ABS sounds perfect for street riding and wet conditions, but it doesn't necessarily stop a bike faster than a non-ABS system. For the aggressive braking required in racing, a non-ABS system can transfer more weight to the front wheel, particularly if the ABS system is set to be very sensitive. The more weight on the front wheel, the bigger the contact patch on the front tire, which leads to greater stopping power. One downside of ABS is that it reduces the feel you get from the brakes because it never allows you to reach the limits of traction.

It's a hotly debated topic, but many believe that a non-ABS system will stop a bike faster in dry conditions, while ABS is better for wet conditions.

There are a few brake caliper manufacturers out there, but Brembo and Nissin are the top choices I've seen around the paddock, along with Tokico. If you're thinking about upgrading, ask around for opinions, especially from riders who've tried a couple of different brands.

As for brake pads, Brembo, Vesrah, EBC, and SBS are the big names. For aggressive braking, a carbon pad will give you more stopping power and wear out less quickly than sintered or non-sintered pads. Personally, I use Vesrah RJL XX pads.

For brake rotors, there are solid, one-piece rotors or floating, two-piece rotors. A floating rotor will allow quicker dissipation of heat, which helps in avoiding pad warping. They are lighter and offer better ability to conform to the brake pads. Because of these advantages, a two-piece rotor is generally preferred.

Brake lines are normally made of rubber straight from the showroom floor, but most people will upgrade them to prevent brake line expansion. Brake fluid can heat up, causing the brake lines to expand and, in the worst case, cause the brake line to rupture. Most upgrades include a switch to steel braided or Kevlar brake lines, which are more reliable under intense conditions.

A master cylinder is responsible for pumping the brake fluid that activates the calipers and pistons. It's a common upgrade to the braking system as it helps increase stopping power, and the most common manufacturer is Brembo.

The lifeblood of your brakes is the brake fluid. I'd personally suggest something that can offer higher temperature thresholds, such as Motul 660.

A lot of advanced riders will use a brake guard. This guard attaches to the end of your front brake-side handlebar and will prevent anything, or anyone, from engaging your front brake while riding in close quarters on the track. It's a small upgrade but can make a big difference in tight situations.

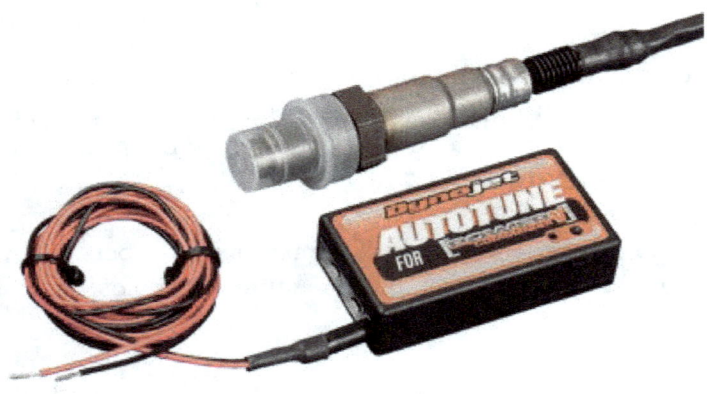

A tuner, also known as a piggyback module, sits on top of the motorcycle's existing hardware and plugs into its sensors and fuel injectors. The tuner box manipulates signals to make the ECU change the fuel/air ratio ignition curves, among other settings. However, tuner boxes can increase strain on the engine, which might cause other parts to fail more quickly. These devices can have an auto-tune feature, allowing them to manage the fuel injectors and O2 sensors, bypassing the ECU, as well as adjusting the engine braking per gear, traction control per gear, launch control, and can even tune per gear for rpm. Some models will also allow you to manually modify any of these settings, but personally, I prefer not to do that. In my opinion, that kind of thing is best left to professionals. Other tuners out there, like Dyno Jet's Power Commander and HealTech, can perform similar functions. From what I've gathered, you can expect a performance increase of 10–20% in horsepower and torque with a proper full exhaust setup, as mentioned earlier.

ECU flashing rewrites the code in the motorcycle's Electronic Control Unit (ECU) to change how it responds to inputs. Many claim that you can improve power by 10–15% and torque by 15–20%, and it can also optimize other performance modifications, like your upgraded exhaust. However, reflashing can carry risks, as it might damage the ECU or other components if the battery voltage drops during the process or if the ECU is updated by the manufacturer. It also prevents the owner from manually adjusting the vehicle after the reflash. A shop can typically perform an ECU reflash for $250–$300.

Throttle bodies

Some people will change out their stock throttle body. This allows you to increase the air flow to your engine when at full throttle. This is generally done while also adding larger fuel injectors to handle this increased air flow. A typical increase in power is 5-25 horsepower is expected.

Throttle cams and kits

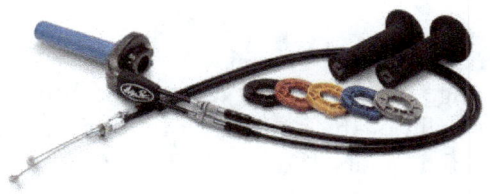

When you twist your throttle, there's a throttle cable that's wrapped around a cam. The cam controls the length of the cable, which in turn tells the throttle body or carburetor how much to open. In simpler terms, this means that when I twist the throttle, the engine will respond faster. So, instead of twisting the throttle all the way to its maximum point, I may only need to twist it halfway. On the track, the most common throttle kits I've seen are from Motion Pro.

Rear-sets

Rear-sets will change your foot peg vertical and horizontal positioning on the bike. This will put the rider in more of a race stance. These are very useful if you find yourself dragging your foot pegs on the ground in corners. Some riders find the change uncomfortable; some think it's more comfortable. Some brands even allow for manual adjustments to fit your riding style.

Tank pads

I find tank pads extremely useful, and they are a relatively inexpensive way to improve your riding. They allow you to stay planted in hard braking when you pin your legs to the tank, preventing you from sliding forward.

Many people who decide to take on this sport will swap their stock fairings with race fairings. These fairings, in theory, are more durable and lighter than the stock ones. They can come painted or unpainted, depending on your preference. However, be very careful when buying from makers without a solid reputation, as they can arrive ill-fitting or badly painted. Personally, I use Sharkskin fairings, which are extremely durable. I've sustained damage to them, and even though they've taken some hits, they haven't split or been in a condition where they couldn't be repaired. In fact, I've always been able to ride on, regardless of the damage. No matter which brand you choose, just make sure they have a good reputation—otherwise, you might find yourself replacing them every time you go down.

A lap timer can help a rider know how fast they are going around a track. Most riders I know use them, and I use one. Some have a built-in GPS sensor that will recognize the track you are on, and some will start timing based on your position on the track relative to a beacon.

Chapter 6 Feeding the Addiction

Introduction

If you're like me, you always want to be the best that you can possibly be. You're hoping that I can impart some wisdom upon you—something, anything—to help you meet your potential. Well, I'll certainly try.

Many great books and YouTube videos have been made on the subject of motorcycle track riding and road racing. I'm a fan of *Life at Lean*, and I've watched his YouTube videos quite often, especially when I was learning to ride on the track. I'd watch while I was riding my stationary bike or on the rowing machine to start my workouts. I also read as much as I could on the subject, devouring content by writers like Keith Code, who wrote *The Soft Science of Racing Motorcycles*, *A Twist of the Wrist I, II*. *Moto GP Performance Riding Techniques* was excellent reading, particularly in the winter months (yes, I'm always thinking of riding, even then!). Other books I feel offer value are Nick Lenatsch's *Sport-Riding Techniques* and *Motorcycle Dynamics* by Vittore Cossalter. Cossalter's book is useful to me in that it details the physics of the motorcycle and how forces act on it and affect it.

Nothing you read will replace getting to the track and riding. Visualizing how you'll ride a particular track is great mental work, but until you actually get out there and practice proper technique—in the elements, with other riders—you'll never be the best you can be. Below, I'll dive into a few topics that outline my experiences, along with some great advice from excellent instructors. You'll get various opinions on each of these topics from different riders, so make sure you listen and ask questions. Every rider has their own technique, and some riders do things vastly differently. Whatever gets you around the track as fast as possible is the goal. One thing that I've learned is that to progress and be 'fast,' you must be on the throttle or the brake. Period. Coasting is a lost opportunity and should tell you that you could have been going faster.

Progressing with your riding techniques by working in steps is how you need to approach your advancement. You'll feel uncomfortable as your riding improves—and that's a good thing. As you get used to performing certain functions, they'll become second nature, and you'll push your boundaries even further, becoming faster with time.

Progress

When you start in this sport, you start at the bottom. This is necessary because whatever you think you know, however well you think you ride, and whatever skills you think you have—throw it all out the window.

If you're not doing this just for fun or to become a better street rider, you're in it to progress in your track riding skills. To progress, you must reset your ego. Think of it as a fun boot camp. Instead of guns and sergeants yelling, you get empathetic instructors guiding you on how to ride on the track at speed. You'll learn proper techniques, like memorizing reference markers, body position, trail braking, downshifting—everything you need to feed your addiction. You also get to ask questions, even "dumb" questions! Odds are, if you're asking it, someone else has the same question.

When I started, I kept as close to the instructors as I could without annoying them. I was talking to them before we went out to ride and afterward. I wanted to be in their hip pocket, towing me around, showing me the proper lines and reference markers. I wanted to impress them but also strove to be better than the others. If that made me a teacher's pet, so be it. I didn't care because I was here to be the best I could be.

I believe that if you have a mindset to succeed, you can progress, no matter what bike you're on. But I don't think you can get any better by showing up to one track day a season. It's like golf. If I play once a year, I shouldn't be surprised if I'm still bad at it every year. You get out of it what you put into it.

If you're in the Novice group, do what you can to stand out. If you feel you can run a faster pace than the others, ask to move. The instructors can always see the slower riders; they don't necessarily know who amongst their group is chomping at the bit to overtake their peers.

When you want to get that bump from the Novice to the Intermediate group, ask the instructor that you're considering it, but you'd like him or her to follow you for a few laps first. This way, they'll tell you you're ready, or you're not ready. Fair enough, right? Keep riding!

In the Zone

The more I ride, the more I've learned to do so, not only by using proper technique, but also by feel. What I mean by that is that at a certain point, I wasn't just on the bike working the controls – grab brake here – roll the throttle there – set up the entry line here – aim your body there. I became part of the bike. I started to feel the tires grip, feel the torque and acceleration, feel the suspension working, and even the subtle sliding. I started becoming aware of not only the track and the riders, but of my bike as I was riding it. I became two riders. Not just the pilot, but also the co-pilot, relaying the nuances of the bike itself so that I could adjust and take note of anything I might need to know to push that limit further.

Take a particular corner, for instance: I'll feel that the rear wheel has plenty of bite for a harder drive out the next lap. I'll feel that my front suspension can handle more braking into the turn. I'll feel the lean angle and tires in the turn, hinting that I can carry more entry speed. I'm constantly gobbling up information, absorbing, and measuring the effects of my actions in these split-second situations. My brain has become an on-board computer, becoming part of the bike, making minute changes to throttle and brake, adjusting body position, tweaking how I'm holding the bike in the turn to increase the contact patch so I can increase corner speed, all of it without necessarily thinking about it. I become emotionless, fearless, calm, extremely focused, and calculated. The culmination of all points of knowledge, thought, and reaction become second nature so that I can absorb everything around me, focused on a single point – to get around that track as fast as I possibly can.

I can only speak for myself about it because I haven't heard anyone quite be able to articulate it. I'd have to imagine that riders everywhere must feel this way. I've felt this in other sports too. Athletes call it being in 'the zone'… You are in this calm bubble feeling everything going on around you, the rush of chaos, the speed, the other riders, but seemingly able to control everything without the thought of doing it. You just naturally seem to be able to create and anticipate, regardless of what's going on around you.

I hope I've described the feeling of 'the zone' adequately because when you feel it, there's nowhere else you'd rather be. It's why this sport is an addiction. I'm always chasing that 'zone'. Always after that perfect lap, that perfect feeling I get.

Picking a Line

There's something known as the 'race line,' the supposed 'fastest' way to complete the track. It's the perfect line, the one you'll want to be on as often as possible. This is the 'happy path,' but it's sometimes not attainable because of other factors at play, including other riders and track conditions. To me, the 'race line' can sometimes feel like a unicorn. It assumes no outside variables will come into play – which is rarely the case. For me, the fastest line is the line I can take to get around the track at that particular time.

This 'race line' depends on hitting the correct 'apex' on each turn and then exiting on the best line to set up for the next turn. For me, the 'apex' is the closest point on the corner where the rider stops the 'turn in' and begins the 'corner exit.' It's normally the part of the corner where you're at your lowest lean angle and have the least traction. At this point, I want all my braking completed so I can begin to get on the throttle.

A straight line may be the shortest distance between two points, but it's not always the fastest. You need to take the line that lets you maximize the speed at which you can exit the corner. The tighter the corner's exit, relative to the apex, the slower I may go and the tighter I need to take the turn. The wider the corner's exit, the more speed I can carry through it, allowing me to sweep wider through the turn. Tight exit turns are often called 'throwaway corners.' In general, you don't gain any time by taking a different line other than the one that lets you get your bike up quick enough to drive out to the next corner. Try to take it with too much speed, and you'll swing wide, blowing the corner. Take it too tight, and you risk losing your front end for a 'low-side.'

I've had to learn this lesson far too many times – yes, even crashing – trying to get through a turn faster than it would allow.

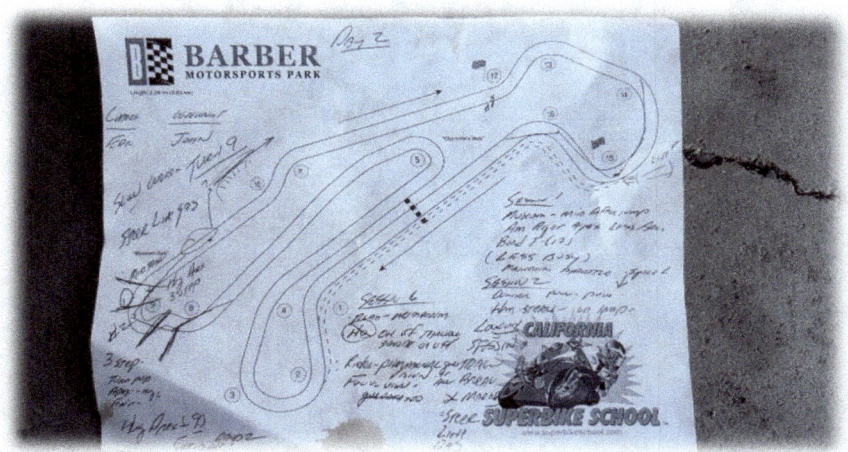

Figure 1 Barber Notes – courtesy of John Burton

A good way to figure out possible race lines on a track is to do a bit of homework beforehand. Print out a picture of the track you're going to ride, grab a pen, and start drawing a line through the track that you think might be the 'race line,' making sure to note the apex points. Then, go ride the track and see if your chosen apexes were correct. Come back to your sheet, make any needed corrections, and start adding other notes like braking and exit markers and turn-in points. These notes can become invaluable the next time you return to that track.

Another good way to prepare for a track is to head over to YouTube. Check out how some riders approach the track, both 'Novice' and 'Advanced.' Pay attention to where they're braking, turning in, and accelerating. Look for trees, telephone poles, and other markers so that when you get on track, you'll at least recognize the environment you're in.

Braking

One thing, among many, that I'm finding really separates the fast riders from those of a slower pace is the ability to brake further into the turn. Fast riders do not coast. If you find yourself coasting for 100 yards, it's a signal to brake later. Having the confidence to carry more speed into a turn is not something that comes naturally. In fact, if you don't approach this step-by-step, bad things can happen. Just because you see a rider brake 200 feet later than you do down the straightaway doesn't mean you should. You'll scare the hell out of yourself and panic if you try to do this all at once. Instead, simply move your braking marker up the track or wait a little bit longer than you normally would to brake. You certainly do not need a racing-caliber braking system, but as you progress in ability, you may want to invest in upgrades that allow you to scrub off speed faster. Even something as simple as changing to a better brake pad can make a big difference.

The act of braking is an art, just like the rest of your track riding. Under all circumstances, when initially starting your braking, remember not to stab or grab the front brake as hard as you can. This is a great way to lock up your front wheel and wish you took out additional insurance on

114

yourself. You should get a shiver up your spine when thinking about it. Most experts agree that all braking needs to be completed before you hit your apex.

Personally, I use my front brakes exclusively, never touching the rear, unless I find myself in the grass. Using your front brake in the grass is a sure way to dump the bike. Outside of using the rear brake to help you slow down faster on a straightaway, more advanced riders will also use their rear brake to help their bike turn quicker. In some cases, your rear brake can also be used to stabilize the bike, shifting the weight from the front to rear in case you are wheelieing or want to get more weight to the rear wheel to increase traction. For instance, you can also use the rear brake going into a downhill turn, shifting more weight to your rear.

Trail Braking

Trail braking is to continue your braking into a corner to scrub off speed, sometimes right up to the apex. Trail braking has a couple of advantages over a brake and coast technique. With this technique, you may start your braking later since, instead of coasting to the apex before you turn the bike in, you'll complete your braking closer to the apex. For example, if you normally finish your braking 100 feet before the apex and then turn into it, consider finishing your braking later, closer to the apex. This technique also allows you to have more weight on the front wheel, making your steering quicker to turn the bike in. Just make sure you're smooth with this technique. You'll want to slowly release the brake as you approach the apex. You don't want to stab or have your brakes at the limit as you tip the bike over, as this could cause you to lose the front tire if you're too greedy with the brake.

Personally, I prefer to trail brake and release the brake just before the apex so I can settle the bike and start to get on the throttle, setting up for my exit drive.

Engine Braking

Engine braking is using your engine to help slow you down by shifting into a lower gear. With engine braking, along with your front and rear brakes, you can achieve impressive stopping power. There's been some debate over whether this should be done, due to the strain it places on your motor and potential effects on rear wheel stability. You need to be careful not to set your gearing too low because your rear wheel will engage in an RPM range that's over the redline, which could harm your motor. Shifting into too low a gear can also cause your rear wheel to lock up, as the motor won't match the speed of the wheel at the pace you were running.

Most modern bikes now have some form of slipper clutch and/or 'auto-blipper' to help prevent the rear wheel from locking up. A slipper clutch keeps the rear wheel from locking by not fully engaging the intended lower gear until the rear wheel can safely engage without locking. Blipping is adding throttle, without being in gear, when the downshift occurs, matching the RPMs of your lower gear to the speed at which your rear wheel will be engaging. You can blip manually without an 'auto-blipper' by quickly adding throttle when your clutch is fully engaged, just before you let it out. You may also try letting out the clutch smoothly, allowing the rear wheel to catch up to the motor's RPMs.

Personally, I use a combination of front wheel braking and engine braking. I'll engage my front brake first and start to downshift just before I enter the turn.

Throttle

"The difference between a track day rider and a professional racer – how quickly and how often full throttle is applied.
Body position, bike lean angle, reference points, corner entry, trail braking, apex, corner exit are all aspects that relate to getting to full throttle safely effectively and often."
Keeping the contact patch at its optimum is important in management of tire wear and maximizing forward progression.
ALL of the above riding techniques, concepts and insights leads too being on FULL THROTTLE!"
John Burton – Lead Instructor

When I think of power, I think of torque, and to me, it's all about how much to apply and when to apply it. How much torque do I have available to use in a corner, at a particular lean angle? How much torque can I apply to the rear wheel without causing it to spin and break loose? And, most importantly, when do I apply this power?

When to get on the throttle and how much to apply will become a personal choice, but I can repeat the unwritten rule that "thou shalt not chop the throttle." The throttle should always be applied smoothly, not abruptly. You have to give the bike a chance to adjust – to allow the weight to transfer to the rear of the bike and to allow all available traction to be used for the torque you're requesting from the rear wheel. I want my rear wheel to grip the pavement, not spin on it. The traction your bike has available will dictate how much throttle you can use.

To me, speed has very little to do with it. The real focus is on available torque that I can safely apply. For example, I can be in a long, sweeping, high-speed corner and have my throttle completely wide open at low, more extreme lean angles. I'm at the top of my powerband with very little torque left to apply, even with limited traction available. At this point, there's very little danger of high-siding, no matter my speed, because any increase in throttle won't yield the torque necessary to break the traction I have at my wheels. On the other end of the spectrum, if I'm at a low, extreme lean angle and I have considerable torque available with very little traction, I can break traction of either the front or rear wheel (normally the rear) with very little throttle engagement. The traction available isn't enough to compensate for the torque I'm transferring to the bike.

So, when do I use this power? As early as possible. Once my line is set, preferably before the apex. Ideally, you don't apply gas at your most extreme lean angle, so I'll start to engage the throttle either just before or after the apex. Getting on the throttle prior to the apex ensures the weight has been transferred to the rear of the bike, and the tire is now locked onto the pavement. At that point, I'm ready to apply more throttle, lift the bike up, and get the hell out of there. Gas and brake. Gas and brake.

Body Position and Turn In

"When you're looking at your riding as a whole, it all starts with the body position. When we watch people get fast, I mean fast, the difference is in the body position vs. bike position. That is the key. Everything is a trickle down from those things. It is the balance between hanging off, bike lean angle, and being on balance. The difference between a 1:25 and a 1:23 is body position."

– Aaron Hardman – Lead Race Instructor

It's something that riders are always working on. Watch a guy pass you, and you'll see how much faster he'll get through a corner. He or she can only do it because their body position allows them the lean angle and traction they need to achieve it.

In my experience, more entry speed into a turn is by far the biggest factor that separates the faster riders from the rest. Watch the MotoGP racers, dragging elbows and knees on the pavement, with their ass completely off the seat. They look like they're carving a line through the turn.

When it comes to corners, my body position is broken down into two major components. The first is my lower body, including my ass, feet, legs, upper torso, and head. The second is what my arms are doing.

Component 1:

- **Ass**: My ass is well off the center of the seat and in the direction of the turn.
- **Feet:** The balls of my feet are almost always on the pegs, pointed either down or away from the pavement. My heels are pressed against the bike.
- **Legs:** My leg on the outside of the turn is planted firmly against the tank. The leg to the inside is hanging off, helping with weight distribution.
- **Upper torso and head:** I aim my upper torso and head toward my intended direction – the apex.

Component 2:

- Arms: My arms are pushing the bike away from me. By keeping the bike more upright, I can get a wider part of the tire onto the pavement, increasing my traction.

Component 1 is responsible for my lean angle. Component 2 is responsible for my tire's contact patch. The faster I want to go in a turn relates directly to the traction limits I have, so I need to balance my lean angle with how far I can keep the bike upright. Ultimately, body position dictates the maximum speed I can take through a given corner.

The important takeaway here is that I want to do all this movement before I get to the apex, as smoothly as possible. Personally, I'd rather misjudge a corner and run wide than adjust too abruptly mid-corner and risk a 'low-side'.

Mid Corner

At this point, I'm, as they say, fully "in it to win it." My mind is made up. My braking is done, my speed is set, I'm on my line, and my body is completely set. There's no room for doubt now. "Thou shalt not perform any mid-corner corrections!" I'm now married to this corner because trying to correct anything will result in surprises—many of which I try to stay far away from. You commit to this corner, you own it.

Most of the downforce pressure from my weight will be on my outside foot. This allows me to relax my inside leg, letting it hang off the bike, shifting even more weight outside the bike. Done correctly, I'll hit that all-important milestone of 'dragging knee', scraping up those knee pucks. I'm not going to lie—it's still a thrill. Touching your knee to the ground is not just exhilarating; it's also a sign you're getting close to your maximum lean angle.

It's absolutely crucial that I stay as smooth as possible at mid-corner. My traction is at its lowest point, so any abrupt braking or throttle use will cause me to 'low side' or 'high side'. I won't deviate from my body position until it's time to start my exit.

When in mid-corner, I'm generally on the throttle just enough to keep the same speed, until I start my corner exit. This is known as 'maintenance throttle.' It allows me to keep my speed steady, as opposed to losing momentum. Not only does this steady the bike, but it also keeps enough weight on the rear wheel for the traction I'll need for a smooth drive out of the turn.

Corner Exit

From mid-corner, I'll start to roll on the throttle. This gradually helps me start to lift the bike up, and as I do, allows more throttle to be applied. The higher the bike comes up, the more throttle I can apply until I'm eventually at full throttle. I aim to use as much throttle—and as much track—as I can to carry more speed, keeping in mind the next corner and the line it requires for the best approach.

The truth is, the throttle is something I still work on. To be honest, there's still a bit of fear in me about applying too much throttle, spinning the rear wheel, and high-siding. It's a healthy fear—one that's probably kept me safe. But I'm always pushing to find the limit of the rear tire as I come out of the turn. How much throttle you can apply on any corner depends on several factors: speed, lean angle, the contact patch, the track, and the tire. More often than not, I'm surprised at how much harder I can drive out with more throttle than I'd thought.

But that's me. I struggle to find those limits. Some riders find those limits faster than others—sometimes to their own detriment. My advice? Be careful. You'll find those limits in your own time.

The Straightaway

This is the point in the track that opens up where I can just pin it, giving it all I've got. I try to use as much track as possible while entering the straightaway, gathering as much speed as I can from my corner exit. I upshift only when I'm high up into the RPMs, at the top of the powerband, and repeat this until I hit my braking point for the next turn. During this stretch, I'm in a fully tucked position—legs and feet in tight, chest on the tank, and head as low as needed to keep my line of sight clear.

Breeeeath…

Seems easy enough, right? We do it every moment of every day. But I remember the first time I caught myself not breathing, holding my breath just before going into corners. It's not great when your heart rate is around 150 bpm, and your brain and muscles are working overtime. Some riders have even admitted to holding their breath through entire sections of the track. I'm no expert, but lightheadedness and cloudy vision are probably not great for a safe track session.

Every now and then, it's smart to check yourself. If it helps, breathe in as you go into a corner, and out as you leave it—just like lifting weights. It might even become a bit meditative, don't you think? Meditating while track riding. Why not? Before long, it'll help set a rhythm, and your body will follow, doing all the things you've taught it to do. You might even find yourself 'in the zone.'

Grattan My Home Track

Grattan Raceway; Belding, Michigan

Grattan?

Isn't that a potato dish?

Funny name aside, this track is definitely what you'd call meat and potatoes. Don't get me wrong; that isn't a bad thing. In fact, I prefer it over the flashiness of a lot of places.

Grattan is an older track with a rich, storied history in track days and racing events. In Michigan, it's considered a 'home track' by both motorcycle and car enthusiasts. Over the years, I've been on many tracks, and I can't think of any that are more technical. The opinion I hear most is, "If you can ride this track, you can ride anywhere." I believe that to be true. Its blind corners, elevation changes, on/off-camber

122

corners, and increasing/decreasing radius turns, along with a sweeper and a 3,200-foot straightaway, will test riders of ALL skill levels on everything from smaller bikes to the high-powered liter bikes. Many pro racers have been here—and still come—to hone their skills.

One thing I love about Grattan is that you can be yourself here. It's a place where meeting friendly people who share the common goal of having fun on the track and helping others achieve that goal is all part of the experience. While that might sum up most tracks, Grattan's got a different vibe. I almost get the feeling folks let their inner child out to play here. They hop on scooters that match their personality, dressed for the day's environment. From Groms, mopeds, electric bikes, and even those quirky one-wheel balance things, people zip around garages from lower paddock to upper paddock, saying howdy to friends from track days past. Big people, small people, tall people, short people, black people, white people, and every color in between—here, we're all friends.

The facility is run by a fantastic team of good-natured people who all appear to be related on some level. If you see a well-lubricated, smiling fella in a minivan, complete with blinking lights and blaring music, driving around at night, you know you've arrived. Come morning, he's sharp as a tack and helps the track staff peel riders and their bikes off the pavement when red flags are flown.

The place has a certain charming, almost back-in-time feel to it. For one, there's a pool area before you even enter the gates, perfect for families, and a fishing pond for the anglers in the group. The original Grattan sign is a large ball on a pole inside the track gates that still lights up at night. If it once had an adjoining drive-in movie theater on the grounds, it wouldn't surprise me.

Nostalgia – Yes, those gas pumps still function

Just around the corner is a bar/restaurant called the Grattan Pub and a party store. Honestly, not sure what else one needs around here, really. The track amenities are basic and include showers and toilets that flush (most of the time). It's far from posh, but let's be real, I'm not there to sample the craft beer or take in a buffet. I'm there to ride, and Grattan definitely has that—no doubt about it.

The grounds, like the track itself, are special, and can be spectacular. The views in the morning over the track, with the settling mist and meandering fog, really are something unique, set against the lush forest backdrop. Sunsets at night bring an explosion of pastels that settle the sun, and they're instantly mesmerizing and relaxing. Just set up a chair and take it in. When night falls, very little light pollution lets the stars shine bright and reveals some of the wonders we miss closer to the city. Assuming it's not thunder-storming, of course.

As for the track itself, it's the sealer that will get your attention. The sealer is used to fill in cracks that occur in the winters. It's everywhere you want to be! Great in the heat, but not so much in the rain. This track is also notorious for being wet in the morning due to the mist that overlays it at night. I simply abhor a wet track. I don't understand how people can bring further risk to themselves or their equipment by riding in the stuff. I suppose if you're here to learn to ride in the rain, it makes sense, but if you're out to improve your game, make sure you at least have a spare set of rain tires ready to mount and balance.

On this track, you have to be fully aware and engaged! Keep your eyeballs looking ahead, down the track. Know your reference points, because by the time you see some of these blind corners, you'll be off the race line, sweeping wide and in the grass—or worse. Riding this track is not the time to ponder your existence in the universe or wonder if your wife is shagging the neighbor while you're here in Belding, Michigan. This track means business, and not being in the moment will mess you up. Still interested? Then read on.

Turn 1 - It's a highly banked right turn off the straightaway. My braking marker is key here as I'll, more than likely, have my throttle pinned until I drop anchor and head to the apex. There's always an 'oh shit' moment here because I'm hauling ass and praying my braking system is up to the task. I'm also praying I still have the balls to throw the bike into a turn I can't see the other side of until I'm well into the apex.

The line for me is from the left side of the straightaway, focusing on the apex. I will downshift from the straightaway from 5th to 3rd, keeping the bike loose, with just enough power to carry me to turn 2. I generally use trail braking into this turn, if it's hot, but will coast at my desired speed if it feels damp.

For your passing pleasure, and if I'm feeling spicy, I find it's a great place to pass people. I can either brake later than the other rider or take a different line to the inside. Then again, I've been passed by riders I swore I just passed, only for them to overtake me on the outside, heading to turn 2. Dealer's choice.

You can take turn 1 with more speed than you think, thanks to its wide and banked path up a hill. Just dip the bike in and throttle up the hill to turn 2. Sounds easy? Nope. This turn is one of the last on the track to warm up for the day, catching the sun last. Oh, and if it rained the night before, you might come across a stream of water, right near the apex, onto your exit drive. Most riders mention a rear-wheel shimmy at full lean. Such is the life of turn 1.

Turn 2 – is somewhat of a blind corner, meaning I'll need to start leaning my bike over before I see it, at the top of the hill. I try to exit this turn so that I'm aimed towards the middle of the track, setting up for my descent downhill into turn 3.

Turn 3 – is a decreasing radius, uphill, blind left turn that banks in the opposite direction of where you're trying to go. It's a tricky beast, no other way to describe it, but if done right, it can be a lot of fun.

John taught me to approach it from the middle of the track and bank left before I see the corner. If, by the grace of God, I've hit my entry marker correctly, I should fall into the apex. I don't get off my throttle here. At lean, I slowly apply more throttle and aim toward the left side of the track, boogie up the hill, and short shift into 3rd gear to set up for turn 4. That short shift lets you shift before reaching the peak power of your bike, preparing for faster things to come.

Turn 4 – is a short, sweeping, blind right-hander that can be approached from the center or outside of the track. I start my lean at the top of the hill, eyes on the apex, and aim for it when I finally see it. If done right, I'll swing wide from the apex to the left side of the track, setting myself up for the hill ahead.

Why did I short-shift into 3rd gear out of turn 3? Because I'm about to start a downhill descent, at full lean, gaining speed fast as I approach the top of a hill—that's why. The last thing I want to do is upshift at full lean. I want to take that hill with my front wheel probably off the ground if I get it right, sticking to the left side, and praying to the 'baby Jesus' once more for a successful entry into turn 5.

Turn 5 – This is a tricky one and a very misunderstood corner. The track designer did an excellent job of messing with our heads here. Almost everyone takes this turn at a much slower speed than needed. When you crest over the hill from turn 4, you're practically flying— sometimes literally—and all you see is green grass ahead.

The typical reaction here is to brake hard before this right-hander. But for me, it's a high-speed turn. I get over the hill, and from the left side of the track, I throw the bike in with all the glory and faith of my racing predecessors. To resist grabbing your brakes after that hill takes some guts, and when you pull it off, you know you're improving as a rider.

Once I'm in the corner, I straighten up the bike, apply throttle, and downshift into 2nd gear. Now, the downshift into 2nd before turn 6 takes some practice. It's all about timing. As you pick up the bike out of turn 5, you'll downshift to 2nd, banking hard left into turn 6. I know, there's a lot going on here, but it's an incredibly fun corner once mastered.

Turns 6 and 7 – Here come the chicanes, and you'll want to get these right to set up for 'The Bowl.' I'll be at full lean, negotiating each turn to the inside, making sure not to swing wide, because I want to set up 'The Bowl' in the middle of the track.

I'll be on throttle the whole way through because these turns are deceptively uphill. My goal here is to brake hard as I enter 'The Bowl.'

Turn 8, aka, **'The Bowl'** – This turn has perplexed me since my very first time riding this track. It's similar to turn 3—a hard left turn, uphill—but instead of sloping away from you, this turn is banked toward you.

My issue with this turn is that my eyes are pointed uphill and to the left, where I'm entering. It's not a comfortable view and really tests the limits of my neck movement. To put it another way, I actually bought a new helmet that's lighter and has better visibility just to handle this one corner. It bugs me that much.

I'll want to exit 'The Bowl' pointed towards the middle of the track as I head uphill towards the sweeper. To be honest, my exit drive here is piss poor. I'm never driving the bike out as hard as I'd like to, and I know this because if I'm following someone faster, they're reaching the top of the hill quicker than I am. But hey, we're all always working on something.

As I start my ascent of the hill, I'll want to short-shift into 3rd gear. Unless you're on a liter bike, you'll want to be in 3rd gear too, as you'll be reaching some very fascinating speeds approaching the sweeper.

'The Sweeper' – it's exactly what it sounds like, and most tracks have them, but I haven't seen one like this. The morning fog has lifted, and suddenly the forest is crystal clear, nearly 20 feet from you as you rush into it at 80+ mph. From the bottom of the bowl and looking up, all you see are trees, and once you crest the hill, the path ahead becomes clear.

Once I reach the top of the hill and shift into 3rd gear, I throttle as much as I can, bank right, and lean into the first part of the sweeper. Even though it's scenic here, this is definitely not the time to enjoy the view. But it is a good time to assess track conditions, since there's quite a bit of sealer on this part. And let me tell you, wet sealer = Bad news.

I won't shut down my throttle at lean but will slowly accelerate until I hit the kink. This kink forces you to lean even further right for a moment before you can start to straighten up and swing out to the left side of the track. As I come out of the lean, I'll increase to full throttle, flying down the hill towards the bus stop.

Now, here's your warning—you'll be flat out, carrying the mail down that hill if your throttle is pinned. With the combined force of your bike's power and gravity, your brakes and braking marker had better be spot on. Every time I brake into the 'Bus Stop' and downshift to second gear, my rear end starts scattering around. It's the nature of the turn for most.

The **'Bus Stop'** – is a **THROWAWAY** corner. I repeat, a **THROWAWAY** corner. I've tried it at every conceivable angle. If there's a faster way through it, show me. It's slow, period. I've even wrecked on this turn trying to cut it in too close. Even my daughter wrecked in this corner.
The best way I know to handle this turn is to enter from the middle of the track, then take a late apex at the unseen white marker, slowly. If you try to rush this one, you'll swing too wide, have a shitty drive out, and probably get passed for your efforts. My advice? Stick to the race line and get through it safely.

I'd also be cruel to not mention that this part of the track, along with turn 1, is one of the slicker parts of the track in the morning or after a rain, so again, just go slow and enjoy the breather for a couple of seconds. You'll definitely need it.

Turns 10a and 10b – These are turns that are quite captivating, but you also may poop your leathers if they're not respected. The designer of this track definitely had a sense of purpose here.

Once I'm out of the 'Bus Stop,' I want to situate myself so I'm pointed straight up the track. I want to do everything I can to get as much speed as possible driving out, tires be damned. I short-shift into 3rd gear in the middle of the hill. It's important to get a clear view of the top of that hill because if you knew what was on the other side, you might just pack it in and go home.

10a has a blind right-hander hiding after the top of the hill, and I tend to take a line that favors the center of the track. Once I get to the top of the hill, I can't see anything but blue sky, so I do what any blind fool would do, which is dive blindly to the right and hope for the best.

My turn-in marker is just before I crest that hill because I want to start my turn-in for 10a before I run out of real estate. When I turn into 10a, I'm looking for a 'depressed' area of pavement marred by scrapes from car suspensions, exhaust systems, and undercarriages. This spot you really can't miss once you start your lean to the inside of the corner.

When you take this line, your suspension will compress. Let the bike unload and quickly bank your bike immediately to the left. It's like a pirouette, like a little ballet!

Once you have your bike on its left side, you'll roll the throttle and aim for the left side entrance of the straightaway. You'll start to pick your screaming bike up, sweeping wide to the right toward the grassy knoll. Being a former racer, Dave said to aim for garage #2, and that's what I do.

Now what's left to do is shift your body position and pin that sucker onto the straightaway, giving her all she's got until you get to turn 1 and repeat this process.

Enjoy!

Epilogue

Lessons in friendship

No fire codes were broken during this gathering, I'm sure 1

There's certainly a sense of camaraderie amongst friends at any track. At Grattan, I've heard stories of people's pit bikes, allegedly, being duct-taped to the garage ceiling and even hoisted up a flagpole. One poor guy, who was quietly sleeping in his van, woke up to his entire van wrapped in plastic wrap. He had to cut his way out and crawl through a window to escape. These pranks are done with love and respect for fellow racers. Imagine if they didn't like you?

Now, I want to introduce you to some people I'll be referencing. It's only fair that you get a good idea of the characters in my track life. They've each been an outsized influence on me as I progress on the track and through life.

Dave Bavol

Dave at the county fair...bless his heart 1

The man, the legend. Where do I even start with Dave? I say this with love because he's one of the most obnoxious, loudest, crudest people I've ever met. But he's also the kindest, most big-hearted, and giving person I've ever had the pleasure to call a friend. We look somewhat alike with our bald heads, but we couldn't be more different in some respects. He's a leader, whereas I follow, at least in this sport.

Dave used to run the tire services for the STT (Sportbike Track Time) organization and keeps coming back for his love of the sport and the relationships he's nurtured over his many years on and off the track. He's ridden both competitively, as an instructor, and for pleasure, for over 30 years. He's currently the pit chief for a Moto America 750 Superbike team, sponsored and owned by STG (Sportbike Track Gear) and ridden by 'Max Van #48.' When I need anything mechanical done, he's my go-to pit crew and chief, helping to piece my bike back together after a crash or with upgrades. The man has forgotten more about riding and fixing bikes than I'll ever know.

Personality-wise, if a demon and an angel had a baby, you'd have Dave. In the situations that matter, the angel always wins out. When I first met him, I thought he put too much sugar in his 'Rice Krispies.' He's got this high-energy vibe—always talking, always moving, rarely sitting still.

131

Working the track, he's like a carnival barker, chatting up anyone and everyone who walks by. He just has this presence. You need the courage to talk to him because it'll be worth it. He's easy to find, too. Just listen for the 80s jams and look for the SpongeBob socks hanging out where the 'kool' kids are.

You either like the man or don't. Dave's got an insult for everyone; if he's giving you grief, don't take it personally. It just means he likes you. Getting razzed by Dave is a compliment that he's thinking of you. Odds are, there's a bit of truth in the ribbing. But underneath all that, he's got a heart of gold. Get to know him, and he'll show you that heart, often. You just need to get over yourself and bask in his twisted glow of friendship.

I wouldn't be at nearly the riding level I am now without Dave. When I first met him, I needed tires, of course. Then I needed to know what pressures I should be using for the day. He'd say, "With how slow you are, does it matter?" If I needed a hand for some small issue that seemed like a big deal to me at the time, I'd get, "Are you sure you're smart enough to ride this bike? Maybe you need to consider another hobby, like knitting. That way you're not a danger to anyone but yourself!" I'd just smile and give him that look that says, "I don't have a clue and need your help."

I don't know exactly what that look is, but he keeps helping me. I think he does because he knows I'll do my best to try and learn. People say, 'help those who help themselves,' and I believe it's true. While I've paid for some of his time (and parts) here and there, he helps me because he saw something in me. He once mentioned he'd never seen anyone go so far so fast. When we first met, I was riding my Daytona 675 in Novice. Once I got my first bump from Novice to Intermediate, Dave genuinely congratulated me and, for once, didn't ridicule me. He knew how hard I'd been working. He took me under his wing, repaying the universe for someone who did the same for him so many years ago. I hope that when I repay the favor, I can do it with as much patience as he's shown me.

Dave has saved my ass more than once—mostly from screwing up something I was trying to fix or maintain. As little as I knew mechanically when I started, he's taught me almost everything I know. Sure, he's helped, but he's also taught me to help myself. He taught me to change the oil, the correct oil to use, swap out tires, remove and install the front forks and rear spring, and, in general, not to be afraid of working on bikes. I don't hesitate anymore to grab a wrench and get to work, either at the track or at home. It's all part of maintaining the bike. Dave would help, but only after I had failed first.

If we're headed to Grattan for the weekend, we'll stop for sushi at Ohana's in Lansing, and if we have time, we'll play some golf. If we're out of town, we'll take in some local events. One year, J.T. and his family invited us to the county fair. A fair with Dave is, well, interesting. Even there, he holds court with the locals, making friends and gathering a crowd. On the way home, I looked in my rearview mirror and noticed what looked like Mickey Mouse ears. A few seconds later, a Harley came blazing past us doing at least 100 mph with a minibike strapped to the back of his sissy bar. I tried to catch him, but the guy was too fast for my Explorer.

Good times, Dave. You're the best, man.

Jeremy Noah

Jeremy Noah 1 He does like to party…

Jeremy was one of the first people I really got to know at the track. He's tall, lanky, and owns a 'Hanshaw'-built Yamaha R6. That bike will keep up with my GSXR, so who knows what kind of magic Hanshaw put into it. The thing about Jeremy is he'll talk himself into thinking he's too slow, when in fact, he's faster than he thinks.

He does 'like to party' and has been nice enough to invite me to some outings with 'Cousin Marty' and his crew. When we first met, he saw the hunger in my eyes and opened up his camper to me for some of the best mac-n-cheese I've ever had. We've also traveled to Nashville together to ride at the Super Speedway, and it was an outstanding trip. He even made room in his trailer and picked me up from my home. Door-to-door service is rare, and when it's offered, you take it!

His main squeeze, Grace, is just as her name suggests—a real class act. She's a very warm person and extremely attentive as Jeremy's pit crew chief. We should all be so lucky.

Jeremy had a serious, season-ending accident at Road America, and to his credit, he got back on that bike and continues to ride. I truly hope you continue this journey with me, buddy. It wouldn't be nearly as fun without you. Our story is still being written as we visit all of the tracks on our bucket lists...

See you soon, buddy.

John Burton

John Burton 1

You can tell a lot about people by the clothes they wear, and I think that gets amplified at this track. John has been an instructor for over 20 years. He is also a Haberdasher! – look it up, kids; I had to.

When John pulls up in his fully outfitted, jumbo-sized Mercedes luxury van, he's dressed to the nines. The man is 'fly.' He could have just stepped out of *GQ* magazine. Custom outfits complete with jacket, vest, pocket watch, fitted shirt, and footwear made from alligator or ostrich— probably worth the price of a couple of slicks, I'm guessing. I don't dare ask. But even a man with such sophisticated taste will immediately strip down to shorts and an old T-shirt, fire up a cigar, and unload to fill his garage with all the toys he needs for a weekend at the track. This includes, but isn't limited to, a small grill, coffee maker, glove and helmet dryers, workbench, lawn chairs, and two Ducatis. One 'Duc' for the grown kids he instructs and one for when he really wants to push himself on the track.

John is an amazing person. He was partly responsible for keeping me in the sport when I got laid off last year. When I called him to let him know I was going to sell the bike, he simply asked, "Are you still having fun?" That's all it took. I soon found another job to support my family (and track addiction) and haven't looked back.

You'd think someone like John, with his elegant style and life experiences, could be snobbish or look down on regular folks. But that's simply not the case. He's down-to-earth and always willing to share his own life and track experiences as you share yours. A couple of years ago, he even invited me to STT's July 4th dinner and made it a point to sit next to me, knowing I'd feel out of place. Maybe he felt bad for me. Maybe he just knew no one would mind. Whatever the reason, I haven't missed that dinner since.

One of the best times I've had on the track was trying to race him. He schooled me in the fine art of braking into the race line, blocking me into corners. If, by some miracle, I got ahead of him with a sneaky inside pass going into the straight, he'd just do it again, humbling me. He teaches by example— as all great coaches do. This guy even convinced me to drink chicken broth in the morning before riding so my body retains the water I put into it. When you see a coach or a person you admire, try to get to know them. It's rare you'll get turned away, and you might just make a friend, as I did.

Thank you, John.

Aaron Hardman

Aaron is an instructor with as many years of competitive and track riding under his belt. He owns a wicked Triumph 675R, and there's not much of it that's stock. Hell, it's not even a 675 once Hanshaw got hold of it (but you didn't hear that from me). With a Hanshaw build, there's no joking around. He's blown past my 750 numerous times, often with a wave as he goes by.

Aaron is my age but looks many years younger. He's svelte, lean, and seems to have the prototypical motorcycle racer's build. He's always quick to help and will talk track—or anything else, for that matter. A former law officer, Aaron now owns a mixed martial arts studio. My guess is that his beautiful wife, Mel—a hell of a cook—prefers his current hours at the dojo over the riskier hours as a cop. I'm also going to assume he's a badass, and I wouldn't want to test my assumption. He'll stare a hole right through you, and I'd hate to see what his punch could do.

He's ridden endurance rallies and is the gatekeeper if you want your race license or your bump to the Advanced group. They don't let just any organization give out race certifications, and he's the guy you better get on the right side of. He's the one who helped me learn what I needed to get my bump from Intermediate to Advanced. I wanted his help because I knew he'd be the one doing the evaluation—and therefore, the toughest critic. As he explained to me, "Be consistent, be predictable, and ride your line. Don't worry about speed. That's last on my list of things to evaluate." You'll hear similar advice if you want to advance out of Novice, too. If you don't pass an evaluation, it's okay. I didn't pass my first one from Novice to Intermediate. If you're not ready, you're not ready. But what you will learn is what you need to work on. There's no harm in that.

Thank you, Aaron, for the time and effort you've put into helping me become a better rider—and for being a friend. Eating your ribs at the annual July 4th get-together is a highlight on my calendar.

Keep smiling, man.

My riding organization

I'd like to give a shout-out to the wonderful people at STT (Sportbike Track Time). No, this book is not an advertisement for their services. It's an account of my experience, and since they've played such a large role in my development, I feel I need to give thanks to various people in the organization who have been **more than** nice enough to help me along the way.

Jamie, the first person from STT that I ever talked to. She has put up with more of my nonsensical questions, reversed and updated more orders, and given me track updates more often than I can count. Jamie, whatever they pay you, it isn't enough.

Owen, STT's north director, who always makes the rider's meeting entertaining and whose wardrobe never deviates from the color black. Dude, **I'm buying you** a pink shirt one day. You, sir, are a gentle giant.

Leah and her husband Richard, who loaned me a set of clip-ons when I crashed for the first time. Leah was my first instructor in Novice and helped me realize that I knew nothing about riding on the track. Letting me sit and enjoy dessert in your finely appointed air-conditioned trailer is always a welcome diversion. Thank you both.

The Troms family. Thank you for your hospitality. Diana, thank you for checking me in on a regular basis with a smile and treating me kindly, as you do everyone. Rob, I miss the blue hair! May your cups always overflow with margaritas.

Thank you, Daniel, for the sushi memories and for humbling me when I think I'm finally 'fast' (I'll catch you soon enough, man). You were instrumental in the garage after my first crash, helping to piece my GSXR750 back together again. **Sometimes,** I think we need a M.A.S.H. unit on-site.

Thank you, Mike, for tutoring me so well in Novice and eventually giving me my bump to Intermediate. You showed great patience with this grasshopper.

And to 'Billy the Kid,' who taught me never to be late for a 1:1, especially when it's 90 degrees outside. I still feel bad about that! Thank you also for taking care of my daughter on her first track day. You helped make her day.

'Baby Enchilada,' who loaned me a siphoning tube to drain the fuel out of my tank—never assume you have the right gas in your tank, and if you question it, get it out of there.

'Thermos Man,' who set my suspension at Nashville Super Speedway. I've never seen a guy simply eyeball a suspension and be so dead-on. It's the best setup I've ever had.

Eric Cell, master of the 'zip-tie,' who taught me the lines at Grattan, forward and reverse, by walking the track. Thank you, Eric; your tutelage when I'm struggling is invaluable.

Adam, thank you for helping restore my bike after my first crash. It was a team effort, and your technical knowledge was spot on. I also appreciate you helping me unload my bike off my tailgate at my first track day at Gingerman. Congratulations on retirement, and keep showing no mercy to the racers that fall behind in your wake.

'Iowa John,' keep on cookin'! Thank you for feeding this orphaned man when no dinner was to be found. I'll strap the feed bag on at your table anytime you offer. Thanks for turning me onto my new pit weapon—a matte black e-scooter. I look forward to many a race around the paddock, after hours, of course.

Last but not least, Richard Harris, owner of STT. Thank you for your hospitality and for beating the snot out of Dave and me on the cornhole boards. I look forward to a rematch!

<u>Next Steps</u>

I've been to quite a few tracks, including Mid-Ohio, Putnam Park, Autobahn, Gingerman, and Barber, all with their own unique qualities and character. I plan to revisit these and capture their essence as I have done with Grattan. In addition, I'll be expanding my track experiences by riding outside the Midwest in my journey to be the best rider I can be. All the information I find useful, I'll log it and determine if it's worthy of sharing in subsequent writings, whether as a book or through other media.

This book has been an experience, and I hope that you picked up some useful information along the way, through my journey in life and on the track.

Thank you for your time.

Bryan Blackburn